Clutch

Satan's Fury MC

by

L. Wilder

Clutch

Satan's Fury MC

Copyright 2016 L. Wilder

All rights reserved.

L. Wilder

www.lwilderbooks.com

Cover Model: Austin Zenere
www.instagram.com/a_zenere5

Cover Design: Mayhem Cover Creations
www.facebook.com/MayhemCoverCreations

Photographer: Rodolfo Martinez
www.rodolfomartinez.com

Editor / Formatter: Daryl Banner
www.facebook.com/darylbannerwriter
www.darylbanner.com

Content Editor: Marci Ponce

Teasers & Banners: Monica Langley Holloway
www.facebook.com/monicalangley.holloway

Personal Assistant: Amanda Faulkner
www.facebook.com/amanda.faulkner.1023

– In The Series –

Catch up with the entire Satan's Fury MC Series today!
All books are FREE with Kindle Unlimited!

Summer Storm (Satan's Fury MC Novella)

Maverick (Satan's Fury MC #1)

Stitch (Satan's Fury MC #2)

Cotton (Satan's Fury MC #3)

Dedication

For all of you

who are looking for your happy ending.

Yours is out there waiting.

Table of Contents

Clutch

Satan's Fury MC
Book 4

Prologue

I've always known anything worth having in this life wasn't gonna come easy. It's just the way it is. As much as it may have sucked at times, nothing's just gonna be handed to you.

To get anything in this world, you'd have to have heart and determination, and my folks made damn well sure I knew it. They were good people ... full of love and grit. I grew up watching my dad bust his balls every day of his life working the line at the local tire factory and doing odd jobs at the garage on the weekends. Whenever we needed extra cash to buy those cool tennis shoes the popular kids were wearing or the name brand shirts my sister was always yammering about, he'd take on a few extra shifts to make sure we could get them. He never complained, not once. Seeing us happy kept him going, and even though he worked hard, he always found time to enjoy life. My mother was the same way. She worked full time as a nurse at our local hospital and kept her house running with a warm meal on the table at night and clean clothes ready for us in the morning—

and she did it all with a smile on her face. I loved how she was always laughing, always finding humor in the little things. Her spirit made our house a home.

My folks loved us, but they worked hard and expected me and my sister to do the same. They had high expectations and accepted nothing less than our best. They wanted us to be happy and have a good life, and believed that good grades and college were the best ways to make that happen for both of us. I did what I could to make them proud, but whenever things got to be hard, I found myself at the foot of my Grandma Pip bitching about my problem of the day. She'd sit there in that old blue rocking chair listening to me gripe as she peered at me over the rims of her bifocals. When I was done complaining, she'd offer me her advice on whatever was bugging me, but she'd sum it up by saying the same thing every single time: "Life ain't always peaches and cream, hon. You're just gonna have to toughen up and make things happen." She'd then tell me to ignore the pain, forget all the obstacles that stood in my way, and fight for what was important to me. I'd try to explain to her that it wasn't that easy, but she never listened, never wanted to hear my excuses. She agreed with my folks that there was only one path that led to a good life, and if you were strong enough to follow it, you'd find happiness.

I'd like to say that following in my parents' footsteps came naturally to me, but it didn't. I was driven and determined, just like them—even more so in some ways. I wanted a good job, a big house, and a fancy car, and I wasn't afraid to work for it. I did what was expected. I started my first job as soon as I turned fifteen, graduated high school with honors, and got a full ride to college with a football scholarship. Everything I thought I wanted was within my reach, but it just didn't feel right. I tried ignoring that gnawing feeling that I was on a path that I really didn't want, but it was no use. I was fighting for something that wasn't meant to be mine. The closer I got to my parents' dreams, I knew in my core it was just that: *their* dreams. I didn't want the highfalutin job or the big fancy house. It all seemed so mundane. I wanted something different, something *more*.

I left college and the good graces of my parents to find my "something more". When I met Cotton and the other brothers of Satan's Fury, I knew I'd found just what I was looking for. Being with them made me feel alive ... really alive for the first time in my life. With them, I found a brotherhood that offered a life that fulfilled my need for adventure, and a sense of belonging that I'd never really known.

It wasn't the life that my parents had expected for me. Hell, it wasn't even the life I'd expected, but I couldn't imagine wanting anything more. That's when I decided that walking away didn't mean I was giving up; to get what I really wanted, I had to be strong enough to know when to let go.

Chapter 1
Olivia

My life was rocking along great. I'd graduated college and had gotten a great job in pharmaceutical sales. I'd moved into an amazing apartment overlooking the city and felt like everything was going my way. I couldn't have been happier, but it didn't last. All it took was one phone call, one traumatic moment, and my world as I knew it shattered down around me.

Three months earlier...

"Hello?" I answered as I rubbed the sleep from my eyes. I sat up in the bed and quickly glanced over to the clock sitting on my bedside table, noticing that it was three o'clock in the morning.

"Olivia? This is Linda Moore." Her breath caught, signaling me that she was trying to keep herself from crying. Linda lived next door to my parents. She and my mother were best friends, and I knew she wouldn't be calling me at this time of night unless something was wrong. The minute she breathed her name, panic washed over me.

I stood up with my heart racing as I asked, "Linda? What's wrong?"

"Oh, sweet girl…" she cried. "I think you need to come over to your parents' house."

"Why? What's going on?" I pushed.

"It's your parents… someone broke in." She hesitated. "Bless their hearts. Someone shot them both, Olivia. Oh, darlin'… your parents were murdered," she sobbed.

After that, all I could hear was static. My heart pounded against my chest as horrifying thoughts took over my mind. My momma… my sweet, precious momma. My dad, my invincible dad, gone. No! No! No! My body turned ice-cold. I couldn't breathe. My skin hurt, my knees buckled, and I fell to the floor. I gripped the phone in my hand, held it to my ear, but I couldn't speak. Thoughts of our house flashed through my mind—the large two-story brick home that I'd grown up in, the very one in which I felt so loved, so safe. When I closed my eyes, I could see my mother standing at the stove, talking incessantly about her day while my father sat back in his recliner and pretended to listen to every word. I could even see her big white Boxer peering in through the front door window, pleading for someone to let her in. I could smell the flowers she'd have sitting on the kitchen table, and I just couldn't fathom anything bad ever happening to her. Then the next instant, unwanted images bombarded my thoughts … the sounds of gunshots exploding through the house, small clouds of smoke drifting down the long hallway to my parents' bedroom, my mother and father lying in their beds in blood-soaked pajamas. Endless horrific visions kept pounding through my mind. Eventually, my thoughts drifted back to that long hallway, and my breath caught when I remembered my brother and sister's rooms were just a few feet away from my parents' room.

I raised myself off the floor and asked, "Linda! What about Charlie and Hadley? Are they okay?"

"I don't know, dear. The police have been looking for them for over an hour, but there's no sign of them."

"Oh my god. I'm coming. I'll be there as soon as I can," I told her as I tried to fight the overwhelming, strangling fear that filled my soul. All I knew or instinctively felt was that I had to find my brother and sister—and I had to find them now. My head was pounding. I couldn't think clearly as my mind raced with so many unimaginable thoughts, but somehow I knew I had to get my clothes on and go.

In a matter of minutes, I was in a pair of sweats and a t-shirt racing my car towards my parent's house. I could barely see through my tears as I drove, but I didn't slow down. I had to get to Hadley and Charlie. They were all I had left. Mom had me when she was still very young. She'd barely finished high school when I came along, and after realizing how difficult it would be to start a family so young, she decided that they should wait before they had any other children. It was almost eleven years later before she got pregnant with Charlie, and Hadley came along two years after him. Even though there was a vast difference in our ages, we were still extremely close. I was thrilled when they were born, and I couldn't imagine my life without them in it.

When I parked the car, I was immediately overwhelmed by all the flashing lights and the people … so many people. It was chaos. The neighbors were all standing in their front yards talking and watching as the police rushed around asking questions and writing their reports. I just stood there astonished, frozen with shock. I couldn't believe that this was all really happening, that it was happening to me, to *my family*.

Everything was a complete blur, until I spotted the paramedics pushing the two long stretchers down the front walkway. Everything fell silent as I watched them open the doors to the ambulance. The breath rushed from my lungs as I watched them carefully load my parents into the back. My feet wouldn't move. I felt frozen, terrified. I wanted to call out to my mom. I needed her to tell me that this was all some terrible mistake. I needed her to tell me that they were okay, that this was just a bad dream, but when the doors of the ambulance slammed shut, I knew that was never going to happen. My mom and dad were gone, and no amount of screaming was going to change that.

I had to find Hadley and Charlie. I had to know if they were okay. The hope that they were still alive was the only thing that was keeping me from falling apart. I headed for the house, carefully slipping past the yellow tape that crisscrossed the front door and stepping inside. I was just about to start up the stairs when I felt someone's hand wrap around my elbow, pulling me back away from the steps as he asked, "Where do you think you are going?"

I looked over my shoulder and immediately caught sight of a large, older man in a policeman's uniform. I took a step back and said, "I'm Olivia Turner. This is my parents' house. I need to find my brother and sister…"

"This is a crime scene, Ms. Turner. You can't just go traipsing through the house interfering with the evidence," he scolded. "You need to wait out front with Officer Stenson. He'll have some questions for you."

I jerked my arm free from his grasp and shouted, "No. I'm not going anywhere. I need to know what the hell is going on. Where are my brother and sister?"

"Ma'am, I know you are upset, but you've got to settle down," he reprimanded.

"And how am I supposed to do that? My parents have been murdered, and I don't know where my brother and sister are. I'm going crazy here. Can't you tell me something? Anything?" I pleaded.

"I wish there was more to tell. From what we can gather, someone broke in around one-thirty this morning. There's no sign of forced entry, so either the door was left unlocked or someone had a key. There are no signs of theft, so it looks like they were here for one reason and one reason only," he clarified.

"To kill my parents?"

"Yes," he answered.

"And Charlie and Hadley? What about them?"

"We haven't been able to locate them. Their beds have been slept in and their clothes are still in the closet, but there's no sign of them anywhere. From the looks of their rooms, whoever killed your parents tried to find them. Their rooms have been turned upside-down." He paused for a minute, then leaned in closer to me as he confessed, "My gut tells me they were able to get away, but there's no real proof of that. You got any idea where they might have gone?"

Hope instantly washed over me. If they were okay, I knew where they were. My mother had a dumbwaiter installed when Hadley was born. She had it placed in the bathroom that was located between their bedrooms, thinking it would help her out with the laundry. Unfortunately, it quickly became a nuisance. My brother and sister loved taking turns hiding inside that creepy thing and inching their way down to the basement. As they got older, they realized that they could take the next step and use the basement window to sneak outside. They'd slip out at all times of the day and night, and it drove my parents crazy. Thankfully, Charlie was only fourteen, so sneaking out usually meant going to the local park around the corner. Hadley would follow him whenever he'd let her, and they'd spend a few hours in their own little imaginary world, playing games and telling stories. I just prayed that they'd managed to get away without getting hurt.

Without checking to see if he was going to follow, I turned from the police officer and rushed out of the front door, running as fast as I could towards the park. It was still dark and the morning fog had started to creep in, making it almost impossible to see. I started calling out their names over and over, praying that one of them might answer. Just before I made it over to the monkey bars, I spotted Charlie sitting on a bench with Hadley resting her head in his lap. Even with his shaggy brown hair covering his eyes, I could still tell that he'd been crying. My heart ached as I watched his hand run up and down Hadley's arm. He was a good big brother, and tonight, he'd gotten her out of that house and kept her out of harm's way all on his own.

I rushed over to him and wrapped my arms around his neck, hugging him tightly as I cried, "Thank god you're both okay. I was worried out of my mind!"

"We're okay … but Mom and Dad …" he started, then stopped when he started to sob.

Still holding him close, I whispered, "I know, sweetie. I'm so sorry you were there when it happened."

"I couldn't save them, Livie. Those men … they were so much bigger than me. I couldn't …"

"Oh no, honey. Don't do that." I leaned back and looked at him as I said, "Charlie, Mom and Dad would've been so proud of you tonight. Don't you know that? You got Hadley out of that house all by yourself. You saved your sister's life and yours. You were so very brave."

He glanced over to me with tears streaming down his handsome face as he sobbed, "I wish I could have done something more. I wanted to ... really, I did. Now they're gone. What are we supposed to do without them?"

"I don't know, Charlie, but we'll figure it out," I assured him.

Reality was starting to set in. We were all alone, and I had no idea who I could turn to. Our grandparents had died years ago and the rest of our family lived hundreds of miles away.

"Livie?" said Hadley with tears filling her eyes.

Her dark hair framed her face, making her porcelain-smooth skin seem to glow against the darkness of the night. She stared at me with those beautiful blue eyes, silently pleading with me to tell her that everything that had happened was just a bad dream. Since I couldn't tell her what she needed to hear, I reached for her, wrapping my arms around her as I held her close to me. I gently ran my hand over the back of her head and said, "It's okay, sweetheart. Everything's going to be okay."

Unfortunately, I was wrong. Everything wasn't okay. The police had several leads, but were never able to identify the men who killed my parents. I tried telling them that the murder had something to do with my father's work, but they wouldn't listen. Everyone knew he owned one of the most prestigious real estate companies in the state, and over the past year, he'd managed to bring in several new developers to restore the downtown area, making it a place where people would actually want to go spend their time and money. When he pushed to bring in a new investment broker, he'd met a great deal of resistance. People were getting angry to the point that it made my mother worry, but my father kept pushing forward. I wasn't sure what exactly triggered the attack, but I quickly discovered they weren't the only ones being targeted.

After the shooting, the kids and I couldn't bear to go back to the house, so I took them home with me. Somehow we managed to make it through the funeral, and the kids were doing their best to adjust to the reality of our new lives. Unfortunately, just a few days after the funeral, I noticed a dark blue minivan following us back to my apartment. At first I thought it was a coincidence, but it was far from it. That damn van could be spotted everywhere I went—work, the grocery store, a friend's house across town—and Charlie even noticed it sitting outside his school building. It was obvious that someone was watching us, but I just didn't know why. When I talked to the police about what we'd seen, they were sympathetic, but there wasn't much they could do since we didn't have the license plate number or even a basic description of the driver. When I came home to find that someone had been in my apartment, I was at my limit, scared and confused, and had no idea what I should do.

Then, things got even worse.

Hadley was on the way to the car rider line when she noticed a strange man watching her. Something about him scared her, so she left the line and ran back towards the school building. When she looked back, she noticed that he was following her. Completely terrified, she rushed to the office and explained what she'd seen to the principal and the secretary. They went to investigate, but the stranger was no longer there. The police were called in too, but once again, they weren't able to do anything to help us.

Feeling completely frustrated, I called the only person that I felt like I could trust: Detective Brakeman. He was the lead officer in charge of my parents' case, and he'd been the only one that seemed to listen.

When I called, he immediately answered. "Hi, Olivia. I was just about to call you. I just heard about what happened at the school. Is Hadley okay?"

"Other than being totally freaked out that someone was after her, she's fine," I told him as I tried to control the tremble in my voice.

"Now, Olivia. We don't even know if this man was really pursuing your sister. It could have been nothing … a parent or a substitute. I know you're traumatized, but like I've said, whoever killed your parents could have easily gotten your siblings too, if that was their aim. Why do you think someone is after your sister?"

"I'm not sure. I was hoping that you could tell me

that. Maybe they think the kids saw something the night my parents were killed."

"Maybe. Has your brother remembered anything else about that night or the two men he saw in the hallway?" he asked.

"No. He's tried, but he hasn't come up with anything new. Honestly, I think he's too upset to think straight. He doesn't feel safe here," I explained. "None of us do."

"I've got units patrolling your apartment by the hour. I'm doing everything I can."

"I know, and I appreciate all that you have been trying to do, but it just isn't enough. It's time to get the kids out of here ... at least until you find the people who murdered my parents."

"Olivia ... just give it some time. If anything else happens with you or the kids ..."

I stopped him before he could continue and asked, "What would you do if you were in my shoes, Detective Brakeman? Hadley and Charlie are all I have left. Would you just *give it some time*?"

He let out a sigh and admitted, "No ... No, I wouldn't. So where do you think you will go?"

"I don't know yet, but I'll think of something," I answered.

"When you figure it out, let me know. I'll do what I can to help," he offered.

"Thank you. I will be in touch as soon as I get us somewhere safe and settled," I promised.

As soon as I got off the phone, I went straight to the bank and liquidated all of our accounts, trying to get my hands on as much cash as I could. On my way home, I stopped by the house to check my parents' safe for any money or jewelry they may have hidden. Luckily, my father had several thousand dollars squirreled away. I took everything that was there, and when I got back to the apartment, I packed us up and we left, leaving our home and everyone we knew behind. I had no idea where I was headed or what I was going to do when I got there. I just knew we couldn't stay in Boston a minute longer.

As soon as I started the car, Hadley started in on me with the questions. "Where are we going?"

I glanced over in her direction, instantly noticing the serious expression on her face. She'd always been one to worry about things, and with everything up in the air, she was more concerned than ever. I shrugged and answered, "I'm not sure yet."

She pulled at the end of her ponytail and pushed on. "If you don't know where we're going, then how are you going to use your GPS?"

"I'm not going to use my GPS."

"Why not?"

"Because I don't know where we are going, Hadley. I guess I'll just figure it out as we go."

She was silent for a minute and then asked, "How are you going to make sure those men don't follow us?"

That was the question I really needed to consider. I

reached in my purse and took out my phone, quickly tossing it out the window. "First, we ditch our cell phones."

"What? No way!" they both shouted simultaneously.

"If these people are looking for us, our phones will be the easiest way for them to track us. We have to get rid of them," I repeated.

"This is so unfair," Charlie pouted.

"You're right. It is totally unfair, but right now I don't have a choice. We can try finding a pawn shop or something tomorrow to get you a new phone under a different name, but for now, toss it," I told him as I motioned towards the window.

With a look of pure agony, he threw the phone out the window. Lastly, with a scowl on her face, Hadley reluctantly did the same. I rolled up the windows and tried to ignore the angry glares I was getting from the kids. It didn't take them long to settle down, and I thought they'd both fallen asleep until Hadley asked, "Are you going to try to get a job whenever we get where we're going?"

"I will, but it won't be like the job I had back at home. Maybe I can find a job as a waitress or a cashier. Maybe both, depending on how much they pay. And I'll have to a find a place for you and Charlie to go to school."

"School?" she groaned. "Why can't we just take a few weeks off?"

"That's not going to happen. I don't want you getting behind. As soon as we get settled, Detective Brakeman is going to do what he can to help you get enrolled. You'll have to use different names, but we will work it out."

"I don't want a different name," she huffed. She pulled her knees up to her chest, covering them with the hem of her oversized sweatshirt, and whined, "This sucks."

"Yep. It sure docs," I agreed. I wanted to come up with some kind of positive spin to put on the situation, but there wasn't one. I couldn't think of one single good thing about any of it.

Hadley turned and stared out the window, giving me her best silent treatment. I left her alone, knowing that she just needed some time, and continued to drive down the East Coast. The kids were exhausted, so after only a couple hours of driving, they both fell sound asleep. It was the first real moment I'd had to myself since my parents were killed. There was always someone around or something that had to be done, so I hadn't really had the time to think about everything that had happened. I hadn't stopped to think about how much I missed my parents or the large, empty hole that was lodged in the center of my heart. I hadn't had time to think about how much it hurt to lose them. I had to push my feelings to the side. I had to learn to forget the rage, the fear, and the sadness before it completely broke me and left me a shattered mess. I had to keep it together for Charlie and Hadley. I was all they had left, and I couldn't let them down.

We were in the middle of the second day of driving when Charlie asked, "We're in North Carolina right?"

"Yeah. I guess we are," I admitted with a smile.

He perked up in his seat and said, "Then we're getting close to Tennessee. We should go there."

"I guess we could. Is there somewhere special you had in mind?"

"Nashville would be cool ... or maybe Memphis. Definitely Memphis. Remember how Dad was always talking about how he wanted to go see Graceland?"

I laughed. "Yeah. I think he mentioned it a time or two."

"I think that's where we should go."

"Okay. We'll give it a shot," I told him as I reached for the map. I decided that it was just as good a time as any for him to see the place where Elvis made his mark, never realizing that the famous city in the south was about to make quite a mark on me as well.

Chapter 2
Clutch

It'd been almost two months since the day I left the club. I'd spent most of that time driving across the country from one city to the next and trying to map out our new distribution route. I'd only been gone a couple of days when Cotton called to give me my new orders. If I was going to be out on the road, he wanted me to make good use of my time.

Even though I was technically working, it'd been good to be out on my own. I needed time away from her, the woman I loved but couldn't have. I needed the silence, some time to let the storm of thoughts settle in my mind. I simply needed time away from Cass and all the constant reminders of what I couldn't have. There were times that I missed the hustle and bustle of the club—the loud music, the sounds of my brothers coming and going at all times of the day and night, the anticipation of what the hell was going to happen next—but being out on the open road had done me good. There was a sweetness to the silence, a peace that only comes from being on a ride. It'd given me time to sort my shit and move on. I couldn't dwell on the past or dream about the future. I had to live in the moment and forget everything else in between. I was ready for a new start, ready to see what was waiting for me around that next curve. I had no idea what the future held. All I knew for certain was that life was a crazy fucking ride, and even though there were no guarantees, I planned on living my life the only way I knew how: wide-open.

I'd had enough of random hotels and the unpredictable spring weather. It was time for me to get to my last stop before heading back home. Just as I'd stopped to fill up my tank, my phone started buzzing. When I checked the screen, I saw that Smokey was calling. He'd been calling off and on since the day I'd left, making sure that I was still alive and well, and he'd catch me up on everything that I'd been missing back at home.

I answered, "What's up, brother?"

"I'm about to lose my damn mind. You up for some company?" he groaned.

Laughing, I said, "And why's that?"

"I don't know, man. Seems like everyone is just in a pissed off mood, and it doesn't help that Henley and Wren are knocked up and moody as hell. Wren is acting all weird and shit and she's just a few weeks along."

Wren was Stitch's ol' lady. He's the club's enforcer and not a man you'd ever want to have a run-in with. When he first met her and her son Wyatt, he fell fast and he fell hard. I wasn't surprised at all when Smokey told me that she was already pregnant. My brother was happy—really happy—and I was glad to hear that he'd found someone to break through that ironclad heart of his.

"Hell, I can't win for losing around here," he went on. "You were always better at dealing with this shit."

"I don't know about that," I scoffed. I'd always been able to get along with just about anyone, but I'm not sure I could handle all the women and their pregnancies any better than Smokey.

"Brother, I don't think I can take much more."

"Don't pout, Smoke. It's beneath you," I taunted.

"Fuck you, asshole." He laughed. "Where'd the road take you today?"

"I'm headed to Missouri. Figured I'd go by and see the folks for a day or two before I head down to Tennessee."

The club had been working with one of our affiliate chapters in Tennessee to broaden our distribution route. It was my job as road captain to secure the new pipeline, finding the safest roads while noting all the bridges and any other possible disturbances that we might encounter along the way. Once I was done, Cotton made arrangements for me to spend a few weeks in Memphis, making sure we had everything sorted before I headed home. While I was there, I'd also be working in their club's garage helping to get them caught up on some car restorations that they'd fallen behind on. Since I'd be staying for several weeks and the clubhouse tended to be a bit rowdy, they arranged for me to stay in one of their apartments downtown. I was expected to be there by the end of the week, but before I headed that way, I needed to stop by and see my mother before she blew a damn gasket. She'd been calling me every other day for the past two months asking when I was going to come see her, and I figured I'd put her off long enough.

"Have fun with that," he heckled. "Think I'd rather stay here with all the raging hormones. Better get going. Going out on a run in the morning. I'll check in with you in a few days. Try to stay out of trouble."

"Always," I answered before hanging up the phone.

I finished filling my tank and headed out to the highway. I made it to Caruthersville before nightfall. Not much had changed in the last four years since I'd been home. All the familiar hangouts were still intact, even those like the Rib Shack that should've been closed down years ago. When I pulled into my parents' driveway, I noticed that all of the lights were on and my mother was standing at the kitchen sink looking out the window. A huge smile spread across her face when she spotted me, and I hadn't even made it off my bike before she was racing down the steps and rushing towards me. The years had been good to her. She was still as beautiful as I remembered, tall and lean with her dark brown hair cut short around her face. Her dark green eyes sparkled as she ran over to me with her arms spread wide.

Once she had me in her arms, she cried, "I can't

believe you're really here."

"Told you I was coming," I teased.

She put her hands on my shoulders, giving me one of her reprimanding glares, and huffed, "Don't get cute with me, Thomas. It's been too long. I've missed you something awful."

I leaned towards her, kissing her lightly on the cheek, and said, "I've missed you too, Mom."

"You know, it wouldn't hurt you to call your mother from time to time and let her know how you're doing," she fussed. Before I had a chance to defend myself, she said, "I've just made a batch of chicken and dumplings. You hungry?"

Choosing to ignore her comment about calling, I smiled and answered, "Hell yeah. I'm always up for your chicken and dumplings."

"Grab your stuff and I'll get you some warmed up," she ordered as she started back towards the house.

"Hey," I called out to her. "Is Dad in the garage?"

She nodded as she pointed to the back door. "He's been out there since he got home from work. Has a project he's been working on. Maybe you could help him out, but don't take too long. I'll have your dinner ready in a few minutes."

"I won't be long," I told her as I got my stuff out of my saddle bag and headed towards the garage. When I walked in, I was welcomed with the view of my father's backside. He was leaning over the hood of a 1946 Ford F1, completely oblivious that I'd even walked up next to him. I glanced over the body of the old beat-up truck, immediately thinking that he'd lost his mind trying to salvage it. It looked like it hadn't been touched in the past fifty years, but if I knew my dad, he'd find a way to get it up and running.

I dropped my bag to the floor and said, "Hey, Pop."

He jolted upright, slamming the top of his head against the hood with a loud clank, then shouted, "Damn it all to hell!"

I chuckled under my breath as I watched him rub his balding head with his calloused hand. When he looked over at me, I pressed my lips together, trying to hold back my laughter. It had been a year since I'd seen him, but he looked the same, just a few extra wrinkles around the eyes.

With his hand still on his head, he barked, "You did that shit on purpose, didn't you?"

Shrugging, I laughed. "Who? *Me?* You know I'd never do anything like that."

He cocked his eyes over in my direction and said, "Wouldn't be the first time you've given me a damn headache. Now, come over here and give your old man a hug." I walked over to him and he gave me a tight squeeze as he said, "Been too long, son."

I took a step back and replied, "Yeah, it has."

"You doing okay?"

"Been making it alright."

He gave me the once-over and said, "You look like hell. Wish you'd think about staying home this go-round. From the sounds of it, things at that club of yours have gotten a little sketchy."

Feeling instantly on the defensive, I retorted, "Things are just fine back at the club, Pops."

"You almost got yourself killed. Things are not fine, Tommy."

Dad always called me Tommy when he was trying to make a point. It always got under my skin, but I tried to just let it go so we didn't have another one of our rounds about the club. "I'm standing here, aren't I? I'm good. Not moving home because I had a run-in with an asshole with a twitchy finger."

"You wouldn't have to worry about assholes with twitchy fingers if you were working here with me." He held up his hands high in surrender as he cackled, "I'm just saying."

I shook my head and answered, "It ain't gonna happen, Pops, so just let it go."

"The invitation is always there. You are welcome here anytime." He gave me a light pat on my shoulder and said, "Let's go inside and get you some dinner and a shower. Your mother made your favorite."

I nodded and followed him into the house. Mom had moved some of the furniture around trying to make the tiny house look a bit bigger, but her effort hadn't made much difference. It still felt small, but it was home. I smelled the dumplings simmering in the kitchen and my stomach promptly started to growl with hunger. I couldn't remember the last time I'd had a real home-cooked meal, so I eagerly walked into the kitchen. I pulled out a chair and sat down at the same round table we had when I was a kid and waited for mom to finish making my plate. As I sat there, I realized it was much quieter than it used to be when I was growing up. I missed the sounds of my sister Molly shouting from her bedroom telling my mom that she'd be there in a minute and the loud rumble of dad's football game blaring from the TV down the hall. There was always some kind of commotion going on around us and sitting there in the silence made me a little homesick for the way things used to be.

Mom placed the steaming bowl of chicken and dumplings in front of me and asked, "You want some sweet tea?"

"Did you make it or did Dad?"

"I did."

I smiled and replied, "Then, yeah. I'll take some of yours."

She laughed as she poured me a large glass. "His isn't *that* bad. He just doesn't put enough sugar in it."

"Mom, it tastes like he made it with a dirty sock and then added a bunch of lemon and sugar so he could hide the funky taste. It's bad, and you know it."

She sat down beside me as she shook her head. "I don't know what he puts in it, but you're right. It is pretty bad," she admitted, leaning forward and placing her elbows on the table to rest her chin in the palms of her hands. She just sat there, silently staring at me as I shoved a huge helping of dumplings into my mouth.

After a few long seconds, I finally said, "Something on your mind, Mom?"

"No. I'm just soaking you in. It does my heart good to be next to you." She smiled. "Don't mind me, honey. You won't understand until you have a child of your own."

"That's not happening anytime soon, so I'll just take your word for it."

Her eyebrows furrowed. "There's no special girl in your life? As handsome as you are, you should have the pick of the litter."

My gut twisted into a knot as Cassidy came flashing through my mind for the first time in weeks. I wanted to keep it that way, so I decided to avoid her question by asking, "How's Pip doing?"

Neither of them had mentioned her in the last few phone calls, and I hadn't seen hide nor tail of her since I'd gotten home. Usually she was right up underneath us making sure everything was as it should be, and not seeing her had me worried that something was wrong.

"She's fine. She locked herself away in her room earlier tonight so she could watch her show without your father interrupting her every five minutes with one of his silly questions."

"She doing okay?"

"I don't know. She's hanging in there. She'll never admit it, but she's had a rough go of it these last few months. She's starting to forget things ... can't remember things that just happened a few days ago. One day, she couldn't remember my name. That one got to her bad. It got me, too. I felt so sorry for her, which only made her mad."

"You think she'll remember me?"

"Only one way to find out." She smiled. "But I feel certain that she will remember you. I mean ... you were always her favorite around here, but I was the one always doing for her. You were the one always whining."

I raised my hand in defense and chuckled. "Hold up! I was talking to her about things, *not whining*. And I actually *listened* to her when she gave advice. That's why she loved me," I boasted.

"You've never listened to anyone, Thomas, and you know it. But she loves you. Always has and always will."

After I took the last bite of my dumplings, I stood up and took the bowl in my hand. "I'm gonna go see her before she goes to bed."

After putting my bowl in the sink, I started for my grandmother's room down the hall. She'd moved in with my folks a couple of years back when her health started to decline. Even though she wasn't as strong as she used to be, she'd never lost her spirit and fussed anytime mom tried to help her. After hearing that she'd become forgetful, I found myself a little uneasy as I tapped on her door. When I walked in, I found her sitting in her favorite recliner with her eyes glued to the television screen. I was surprised to see how frail and weak she looked. Her skin had become almost translucent, and dark veins and bruises covered her thin, frail arms. I'd seen lots of old people throughout my life, but I'd never thought of my Grandma Pip as old or elderly until that moment. It pained me to see her look so feeble and weak. When she noticed me standing in the doorway, her eyes lit up and a wide smile spread across her face. She remembered me.

"Thomas! Is that really you?" she beamed.

"Yeah, Pip. It's me."

"Well, it's about damn time. I thought you'd forgotten about me. I was beginning to think the next time I saw you would be at my funeral," she teased.

I leaned over her and kissed her lightly on the forehead. "Ah, don't be like that. You know I could never forget about my favorite gal. Besides, you'll probably outlive us all."

"God, I hope not. I'm ready whenever the good Lord's willing."

I sat down beside her. "It's good to see you. How are you doing?"

"From the looks of it, I'm doing better than you," she scoffed. "What's with the sad eyes and that hair? Looks like you haven't been to the barber in months."

I ran my hands through my hair, brushing the long strands from my eyes. "Just tired. I've been on the road for a while."

She frowned sternly. "Don't go trying to pull the

wool over my eyes, young man. I may not be as keen as I used to be, but I always know when you got something weighing on you. And from the looks of it, you haven't gotten a hold of it yet."

I leaned back in my chair and spent the next half-hour telling her everything that had transpired with Cassidy—how I'd fallen head over heels for her even though I knew she was in love with someone else … and that someone else just so happened to be the president of my club. I explained my reasons for leaving and told her that I'd take the last few weeks to sort through my shit, but when I looked at her, I could see the wheels turning in the back of her mind.

She sat quietly, listening to my entire story, only nodding from time to time to let me know that she was paying close attention to everything I was saying. Once I was done, she sat there staring at me intently as she thought about everything I'd said. Finally, she eased herself forward, looking at me square in the eye, and proclaimed, "Not so sure you really loved that girl, Thomas. I mean, it's obvious that you cared about her—probably cared a great deal for her. But loved her? No … I'm not so sure about *that*."

"I loved her. There's no doubt in my mind."

"No, Thomas. Not this girl. She wasn't the one. You'd know it if she was. When you find the girl that grabs ahold of your heart and holds on so tight that it makes you feel weak yet stronger at the same time … a girl that captivates your every thought, your heart and your *soul*, to the point that you feel like you can't breathe without her ... when you actually *ache* for this woman, *then* you are in love, Thomas. And when you find a love like that, you don't walk away from it. You fight for it. No matter what it takes, you fight for that love and you hold on to it with everything you've got."

Chapter 3
Olivia

I banged on Charlie's door for the second time and shouted, "Let's go! Move it or lose it. We're gonna be late!"

"I know! I'm coming!" he grumbled.

I scurried down the hall while tugging my hair into a ponytail and called out to Hadley, "You've got three minutes, squirt! We need to get rolling."

I looked over at the clock, and it seemed to be mocking me as I rushed around gathering the kids' backpacks and lunches. No matter how hard I tried, our mornings were always hectic. Mainly because I was always anxious and pushed them to hurry up knowing that if we were late in the morning, even by just a few minutes, we would be scrambling for the rest of the day. It didn't matter how hard I tried to get us caught back up; something always kept dragging us back down.

"Can't we just take the bus today?" Hadley whined. "I've still got some math homework to finish."

"You know the answer to that. Now, grab your stuff and let's go. Louise will be leaving in five minutes." I grabbed my purse and headed for the diner. Before I closed the door, I yelled, "I'll meet you downstairs. I've got to go clock in!"

When I walked into the small diner, I wasn't surprised to see that every seat had already been taken and there was a line out the door. The breakfast rush started early and didn't let up until late in the afternoon. It had taken some time, but I was finally getting used to the nonstop stream of customers that came to eat at Daisy Mae's. It was located in the middle of downtown Memphis and known for having the best lunches in town, so it was always packed. I was constantly on the move from the minute I clocked in until just before closing every night.

At first it was hard to manage all my hours at work. I needed the hours, so I managed to convince Louise to let me work more than one shift several days during the week, but that meant I had even less time with the kids. When they weren't in school, they were either stuck waiting for me in the hotel room or sitting in one of the back booths doing their homework. They were miserable, and honestly, I was worse off than they were. I hated not being with them, especially after all we'd been through, but I finally lucked out when the cook Cyrus told me about an apartment above the diner that was for rent. Apparently, he was friends with the owner, and after putting a good word in for me, he was able to get me a good deal on it. When I first saw it, I was surprised by how small it was, but I couldn't complain;

it was something I could actually afford, and it was even furnished. Well, partly furnished. After paying the first two month's rent upfront, we were still doing okay, so I splurged a bit and bought the kids some new mattresses and some bedding, along with a few odds and ends to make it feel more like home.

I was adjusting my apron when Cyrus stuck his head out of the small serving window and shouted, "Louise is waiting in the car out back."

"Shit," I mumbled under my breath.

Louise took her grandkids to school each morning and I was thrilled the day she'd actually volunteered to take Charlie and Hadley along with them. There was just one catch: she wasn't one to wait around. If we were late, the kids would miss their safest way to school. She had her positives, but overall, she was a real piece of work. I wasn't sure if she actually owned the diner, but she ran it like she did. She was much older than her brother Cyrus with a wide girth and a constant snarl, and she was quick to remind everyone that she was the one in charge in and out of the diner. She expected things to be run a certain way—*her way*—and she was quick to crawl up your ass if you screwed up. I was just about to rush back upstairs to fuss at the kids when they both came up behind me.

I let out a sigh of relief. "Louise is already waiting for you out back."

"Of course she is," Charlie groaned. He was wearing a pair of jeans and a collared shirt with his baseball cap pulled down low over his eyes.

"Hey." When he turned back to look at me, I smiled and said, "Hope you have a good day."

He rolled his eyes and sassed, "Whatever."

Normally he was such a sweet kid, always trying to do what he could to help when things got tough. In the mornings, he just couldn't help himself, and the grumpy, hormonal teenager came roaring to life. I tried to be understanding. He and his sister had been through so much, so most mornings, I would just ignore it and hope that he'd be better in the afternoon.

I waved goodbye, but he just ignored me and walked out of the back door. Noting her brother's bad mood, Hadley gave me a sympathetic look and said, "Hope you have a good day, too. See you after school."

"Okay. Check ya later, squirt." I smiled and watched as she followed her brother out to meet Louise.

As soon as they were gone, my morning turned into a blur. Customers kept rolling in one after the other, and by the time my break rolled around, I was exhausted. My feet were killing me and the muscles in my legs were throbbing as I took my cup of coffee over to one of the empty booths in the back of the diner and sat down. Thankfully, my spirits were lifted as soon as I counted up my tips for the day. All things considered, I was doing alright. With Detective Brakeman's help, I'd gotten the kids enrolled into a good school and found us a safe place to stay.

I was still worried that trouble would find us, but

after talking with Cyrus, I felt better about the situation. I hadn't been working at the diner long when he approached me. While Louise seemed tough as nails, Cyrus had a softer side to him. He was a big guy, tall and burly, but he had a sweet smile. He was handsome with his dark hair and coal black eyes, and I liked the little gray bristles in his goatee. Apparently he'd been watching me with the kids and knew something was up, but he didn't ask questions. He just slipped me a card with a strange phone number on it. He told me to call it if I ever ran into any trouble, day or night. He promised that I was safe there at the diner, and I believed him … at least for the time being.

When my break was over, I went to the kitchen to gather up the day's trash and headed out back. I walked out into the alley, but stopped in my tracks when I found a man sifting through the dumpster. When he saw me, he stopped moving and just stood there, frozen in place. He was dirty, covered in dark soot from head to toe, and his clothes were all tattered and torn. The temperature had dropped over the past couple of days, and I knew he had to be freezing. He was a mess, but it wasn't his appearance that got to me. It was the deep sadness in his eyes that tugged at my heart.

The large bags of garbage were getting heavy in my hands, so I took a step forward, doing my best not to scare him as I headed towards the dumpster. Once I got closer, he took a step back and said, "Umm … My name's Sam. Me and Cyrus go way back … and he said it'd be okay for me to come by after lunch from time to time."

I'm not sure what it was, but something about the kindness in his voice drew me to him. Without thinking, I smiled and stammered, "No need to rush off. Why don't you let me get you something to eat. Maybe a burger and a cup of coffee? My treat."

His eyes dropped to the ground as he answered, "Better not do that. I don't think Louise would like it."

"Let me worry about Louise. Besides, the lunch rush is over. No one will even notice that you're there."

"You sure?"

"I'm positive." I tossed the garbage bags into the dumpster and headed back towards the door. When I stepped into the diner, I looked back and I was pleased to see that he was following me. I led him over to the corner booth in the back of the restaurant where I'd always taken my break. It was off to the side, and I hoped it would limit the amount of stares he'd get being there.

Once he was settled, I asked, "What do you want on your burger?"

"Anything is fine." He smiled.

"I'll be back in a minute with your coffee. Let me know if I can get you anything else."

When I put his order in, Cyrus glanced over at my guest and then turned back to me with a disapproving look, but he didn't say a word. I decided to just ignore him and reached for the pot of coffee. I filled the cup full and took it over to the stranger. Without adding sugar or cream, he took the warm drink in his hand and brought it up to his mouth for a long drink. I was about to head back to the kitchen for his food when he pointed to the name tag on my uniform and asked, "Your name's really Hazel?"

I was just about to tell him my real name when Hadley and Charlie walked into the diner, reminding me that I couldn't trust anyone, not even a homeless guy I'd found rummaging through a dumpster. I smiled and answered, "Afraid so. I was named after my grandmother. What about you? What's your name? Do you live around here?" The words were out of my mouth before I'd had time to even think.

"I guess you could say that. I've lived in Tennessee my whole life. Grew up a few miles from here. Traveled all around the world while I was in the service, but always felt like this was my home."

"You were in the service?"

"Over thirty years in the navy. Some of the best years of my life … some of the worst, too."

"Maybe you could tell me all about it someday." I smiled.

"Sure. I'd like that." He beamed.

"Me, too. I'll be right back with your lunch," I told him as I headed over to the front counter to say hi to the kids.

Before I even had a chance to speak, Charlie groaned, "I'm starving. They had some kind of noodle crap for lunch today and it sucked."

"Yeah, I'm hungry, too," Hadley chimed in, giving me one of her pouting looks. "Can we get something to eat?"

"Sure thing. I'll have Cyrus make you both a sandwich." While reaching for Sam's burger, I turned to Cyrus and said, "Need a couple of club sandwiches for the kids."

As I headed towards the back tables, I heard Cyrus say, "Those kids eat more than I do."

I placed Sam's burger down on the table and smiled as I watched him study his food. "There you go. Do you need anything else? More coffee or a soda?"

He shook his head as he said, "I'm good. Thank you."

"No problem. I hope you enjoy it." I smiled and headed back over to the kids. I was going to check to see if their sandwiches were ready, but stopped cold when I saw a man standing at the front door of the diner.

He was like no man I'd ever seen before—rugged, fierce, and sexy as hell. The mere sight of him caught my breath, and no matter how hard I tried, I couldn't pull myself away from those gorgeous dark green eyes. I'd seen my share of bikers come through the bar, but he was different—different in a good way. His leather jacket and long, shaggy hair made him look a bit intimidating, like one of those rough don't-mess-with-me kind of men, but I didn't feel threatened by him—

not in the least. Instead, I felt a strange pull towards him. I found myself wanting to get closer to him, to run my hand across the bristles of his two-day-old beard.

When I felt my heart rate quicken, I chastised myself. What was I thinking, getting worked up over some man? Especially a man like him. I wasn't the kind of girl that was interested in a roughneck biker, and it ticked me off that I'd even given him a second look.

My chagrin worsened as I watched him stroll over to the counter and sit down next to Charlie. Damn. I didn't want him anywhere close to my brother or sister. Before I could go over to Charlie and tell him to move, Louise came rushing out of the kitchen and headed straight for the mysterious stranger. She smiled and started talking to him like they were old friends. Being too curious for my own good, I stepped closer, pretending to check on my other customers as I eavesdropped on their conversation.

"I have the keys to your apartment in my office," Louise told him. "You want a bite to eat while you're here?"

"Yeah, that'd be good. Gus said you had one of the best burgers in town." His voice was low and husky. I found myself wanting to hear him talk again, which only made me more annoyed with myself.

"One of the best? No, no darlin'. We *are* the best," Louise corrected him. "The apartment is right upstairs. It's the second door on the left. Gus made sure everything was ready for you. I put clean sheets on the bed this morning. I'll be right back with your keys," she told him before she headed to the back.

I couldn't believe what I'd just heard. He was going to be living next door! The guy hadn't even spoken to me—and probably never would—but just the thought of him living next door made my frustration level hit an all-time high. I had no idea why I felt so intensely exasperated with his presence. All I knew was that my displeasure was clashing with my newfound raging libido.

When she placed the keys in his hand, he said, "Thanks, Louise. I really appreciate it."

"No problem. And, darlin', you can come by anytime for a bite to eat. It's on the house."

I quickly turned around, looking for anyone that was as surprised as I was by Louise's offer, but no one even seemed to be paying attention. I glared at the man's back, wanting more than ever to thump him right in the head just for being there. After staring at him for a few seconds longer, I decided that a bruising nipple-twist would be a better form of torture for the man who just invaded my thoughts and territory. I was smiling at the thought when Cyrus yelled, "Order up!"

I hurried over to the serving window, reaching quickly for the kids' sandwiches before Cyrus had a chance to scream out again. I placed the plates on the counter in front of them. Without saying a word, they both began stuffing their mouths like they hadn't eaten in days. I refilled their glasses of tea, then returned to check on Sam.

When I got back to his table, his plate was clean and his cup was empty. A huge smile spread across his face when he said, "Best meal I've had in a while."

"Glad you liked it," I answered.

He stood up to leave and softly said, "Mighty nice of you to feed an old fool like me. I owe you one."

"Don't give it a second thought. I was glad to do it."

Once he'd gotten up and headed towards the back door, I picked up his receipt to see how much I owed for his lunch, then reached into my pocket for my tip money and placed it on the table. I thought back to the way Sam had smiled at me before he left and was amazed at how something so small could make me feel so good. I wanted to help him in some way, but I was still struggling to get my feet on the ground. I could only hope that someday I'd be able to do more.

Chapter 4
Clutch

I'd only been at the house for a couple of days when I'd gotten the call from Cotton. He'd given me free reign for weeks, but his patience was wearing thin and it was time for me to get to Memphis. After saying my goodbyes to my folks, I gathered up my shit and got on the road. I'd made it into Memphis well before dark, giving me plenty of time to get settled before my meeting with Gus the following morning. When Cotton called, he gave me an address to a diner where I was supposed to meet up with Louise. She had all the info on where I'd be staying while I was in town.

Louise was the VP's ol' lady and ran a diner as one of their fronts for the club. Her brother Cyrus was also a member and helped her out by doing all the cooking at the diner. When I pulled up to the address that Cotton had given me, I was a little shocked. I'm not sure what I was expecting, but seeing the name of Daisy Mae's plastered on the outside wasn't it. When I walked through the front door, I quickly realized it wasn't your typical burger joint. Pictures of Elvis, B.B. King, Morgan Freeman, and other famous people from Memphis were plastered all over the walls, and a low blues melody was playing from the jukebox. The few people that were sitting in the booths didn't look like they were in any rush to leave as they sat there talking and drinking their cups of coffee.

I made my way over to the front counter and sat down on one of the empty stools. I'd barely gotten settled when Louise came out to meet me. She quickly gave me the rundown of the apartment and where it was located, and after she'd given me the key, she brought me out a plate full of fries and a burger big enough for two people. I'd just taken my first bite when I overheard the kids next to me arguing.

"Scoot over. You keep hitting me with your stupid elbow!" the sister grumbled.

"You scoot over. You're the one that's all up underneath me, smart one," the boy told her with sarcasm. He was a big kid, around fifteen or sixteen years old, where she was a bit younger, maybe twelve or so.

She gave her brother an overstated eye-roll, like a typical teenager, and grumbled, "You are such a jerk, and you look like an avocado."

"An avocado? Really? You're so stupid it's not even funny."

"Well, you're stupider because you have the brains of an *avocado*," she snapped back.

"Would you please just stop talking? Every time you open your mouth, you say something stupid."

She flipped him the bird and then sassed, "*Char-lie*. How's that for saying something stupid?"

"Uhh … give me a break," he growled under his breath. I smiled, remembering how Molly and I used to argue the same way.

I was reaching for my glass of tea when the boy turned to me and asked, "You got a sister?"

"I do," I answered.

"You want another one?" he offered.

"Nah, man. One is plenty," I laughed. "Hang in there. It gets better."

He glanced back over to his sister, seeing that she was glaring at him with an evil eye, and said, "It better, or I'm gonna lock her in the damn closet."

"Livie! He's saying mean stuff about me again," the sister called out to one of the waitresses. She was saying goodbye to one of her customers in the back of the diner. He looked like he'd seen better times, and I watched as she dug in her apron and pulled money out of her pocket to cover the tab. When she didn't answer, the sister shouted again, "Livie!"

The waitress's eyes grew wide as she looked over at the young girl. The brother then jabbed her in the side with his elbow and mumbled something under his breath. The sister's face flushed red, and then she looked up to him and whispered, "I forgot."

"You can't forget," he told her sternly. "Ever."

She looked down at her lap. "Okay."

When the waitress approached the counter, the young girl turned to her and whispered, "I'm sorry. I wasn't thinking."

The waitress leaned over her and smiled as she softly said, "It's okay. I don't think anyone was paying attention."

The waitress looked over to me for just a brief moment, but it was long enough for me to wonder what she was doing working at a biker's diner. It was plain to see that she was no club girl. I glanced over at the tag on her uniform and read the name Hazel and immediately thought she didn't look like any Hazel I'd ever seen. I stared at her for a moment, trying to figure her out. She was a beauty, even with the fear and pain that lurked behind her eyes. Her uniform was simple, plain white with a dark blue apron tied around her waist, and showed off the perfect curves of her figure. Shades of red flowed through her long, dark brown hair enhancing the green in her hazel colored eyes, and it made me think that maybe her name suited her after all.

I continued to eat my burger, and even though I wasn't intentionally listening to their conversation, I overheard Hazel tell the kids to go upstairs and start their homework. Once they'd left, she started gathering up their dishes. Before she turned to go, I asked, "Your name Hazel?"

She glanced down at her name tag and mumbled, "Mmm-hmm."

"So, you got a place upstairs, too."

"I do," she clipped.

Ignoring her obvious aggravation, I announced, "Looks like we're going to be neighbors."

She stopped and, after letting out a frustrated sigh, she answered, "Looks that way. And just so you know … the walls are thin. Please try to remember there are two kids living next door."

I nodded and said, "I'll keep that in mind."

"I'd appreciate it."

"Those your kids?"

Her eyebrows furrowed with a look of irritation as she answered, "No, Einstein. Those are *not* my kids."

What the hell? I held my hands up as I shrugged. "My bad. Just asking. The little girl looks a lot like you, so I figured you were related."

"The little girl … Cindy … is my *sister*, not my daughter," she snapped, "and the boy David is my *brother*, not my son."

She drew her words out slowly, making her point more smart-ass than I deemed necessary, and on top of that, she was lying. She didn't even bat an eye when she said the boy's name was David. I'd already heard his sister call him Charlie, so I knew right away she was hiding something.

I winked and said, "Got it. Thanks for clearing that up, doll."

"Whatever," she snarled and took the last of the dishes in her hands.

Clutch

Hell, she was a spitfire, with her sharp temper and fiery tongue, but there was something more hidden behind that protective wall she'd put up. I knew I didn't have time to get wrapped up in a woman like that, but I found myself glancing back over to the kitchen door, hoping that I might catch one more glimpse of her before I left. When she didn't show, I dropped a twenty-dollar bill on the table to cover my bill and tip and headed upstairs. I needed to get settled before my meeting with Gus in the morning.

When I got upstairs, it wasn't anything fancy, but it was clean and the furniture was decent. It was on the small side, just two bedrooms, and as I walked through it, I wondered how my neighbor managed to find room for two teenage kids and herself. On my way downstairs, I walked by my neighbor's door and heard the sound of a familiar video game roaring through the thin walls, making a smile spread across my face when I thought about Dusty playing the same game whenever he was at the clubhouse. Letting go of the memory, I went on down to my bike, and after I got my bags and map, I headed back upstairs. Once I had everything put away, I spread the large map across the kitchen table. I spent the next few hours plotting the mileage from each of our drop-off and pick-up locations along the route.

I'd just about finished logging all the information for Gus when my burner started buzzing. It was a message from Cotton.

Cotton:

You find the diner?

Me:

Yeah. I'm good.

Cotton:

That's what I wanted to hear.

Report back to me as soon as you're done with the meet.

Me:

Will do.

Cotton:

Be careful.

Me:

Always.

Leaving the map spread out across the small kitchen table, I tossed my phone onto the counter and walked over to the sofa. I sat down on the soft leather cushions and reached for the TV remote. Leaning back and propping my feet up on the coffee table, I started flipping through the sports channels. I'd only been sitting there a few minutes when my eyelids grew heavy and I drifted off to sleep.

I'd been asleep for less than an hour when I heard a loud ruckus coming from next door. When I heard a woman's screams, I shot up from the sofa and rushed out into the hall. The screams continued over and over again, but I couldn't make out what she was saying. I was worried something was wrong, so I pounded on the door. Seconds later, the young girl from the diner opened the door with a startled look on her face.

"Shit! Shit! Shit!" Hazel screamed from the back of the apartment. "Get me a wrench or something!! Hurry!"

"Hey... umm ... something's wrong in the bathroom," the girl explained. "Umm... David is trying to help her, but ..."

"Mind if I have a look?" I asked.

"Yeah, but she's gonna be really mad that I let you in," she frowned.

"Let me worry about that," I told her as I headed towards the bathroom.

When I walked into the small dilapidated bathroom, it took me a second to register what I was seeing. Between all the screaming and the water, it was fucking chaos. The showerhead had broken off from the wall and water was spewing all over the room. With one hand, Hazel had a bath towel covering the huge gaping hole in the wall while her hand continuously turned the faucet knob round and round in a failed attempt to turn off the water. Nothing she was doing was working, not even a little bit, and she was drenched from head to toe. She turned with her mouth open, ready to scream again, and a look of pure horror crossed her face when she noticed me standing in the doorway.

David came rushing up behind me with a wrench in his hand. I took it from him and said, "Thanks, buddy."

I walked over to the tub and knelt by the faucet. After removing the cheap plastic covering, I used the wrench to twist the water off. As soon as the water stopped gushing from the wall, the room fell silent. Still kneeling down, I glanced up at her, but when I noticed her white t-shirt was completely soaked, I quickly turned away. The last thing I needed was her seeing the smile that inched across my face when I saw her perfect breasts beneath the wet fabric. Damn. Damn it all to hell. Seeing her standing there looking so vulnerable and downright beautiful stirred something inside of me that I hadn't expected to feel.

"Exactly what are you doing here?" she sneered.

Throwing her attitude right back at her, I stood up and growled, "Doing whatever it takes to make you stop making so much damn racket. The walls are thin, remember? Some of us are actually trying to sleep around here."

Her cheeks blushed red as she stumbled, "I'm umm ..."

I crossed my arms and, with a raised eyebrow, said, "This is where you say *thank you*."

She cut her eyes at me and spat, "Thank you."

"You're welcome. I'll come back after work tomorrow to fix the showerhead. Just leave it for now."

"No. I'll just tell Louise. She'll get someone to—"

"I told you I'd fix it tomorrow," I snapped as I started towards the door. "Don't want to take a chance on someone screwing it up." Before I left the room, I turned to her and said, "And just so we're clear: you were right about the thin walls, and you scream like a dying hyena."

Chapter 5
Olivia

I couldn't sleep. I wanted to blame the uncomfortable sofa for my insomnia, but I knew the lumpy cushions weren't at fault … at least not this time. Every time I closed my eyes, he was there: my too-hot-for-his-own-good neighbor, the man of my dreams and my worst nightmares wrapped into one. As much as I wanted to, I couldn't get him out of my head. I should have been grateful that he'd come and saved us from a complete disaster, but I wasn't. Instead, I was just plain mad. I couldn't believe he just barged into my apartment looking all disheveled and sexy as hell while I looked like a total mess. I could feel the heat crawl up my face when I thought about that sexy little smirk that crossed his face when he glanced up at my wet chest. Jerk. Then to make matters even worse, he had the nerve to say that I sound like a dying hyena. I had never, nor would I ever, sound like a hyena—dying or otherwise. It was ludicrous, all of it. I would have eventually figured out how to turn the stupid water off. I was just flustered … and wet. I wasn't thinking straight.

I sure as hell didn't need him coming in there making me feel like a complete pathetic moron, but he did.

I was lying there still fuming when Hadley walked into the living room. She came over to the edge of the sofa. "Can I lie down with you for a little while?"

"Sure, sweetheart." I pulled back the covers and made room for her next to me. Once she was settled, I asked, "Why aren't you sleeping?"

"I had a bad dream."

"You want to tell me about it?" I asked as I slipped my arm under her head, cradling her next to me.

She nestled a little closer. "It was another one about Momma and Daddy. We were at home watching a movie and it was dark. We were all sitting there together when those men came in to get us, but this time they got Charlie and me, too."

"It was just a dream, sweetie. I'm not going to let anything happen to you or your brother."

"I know," she whispered. Her little body trembled in my arms as she began to cry, making my heart ache for her. As hard as I was trying, I knew it wasn't enough. She'd been through so much, and with all the changes in our lives, she hadn't had a chance to mourn the loss of our parents. None of us had, and with all of my hours at work, I hadn't been there for her like I'd needed to be. I was too busy just trying to keep us afloat, and I hadn't been able to spend time with her or Charlie. I had to figure something out—and soon. I gently ran my fingers through her hair and kissed her lightly on the back of her head, quietly holding her as she continued to cry. "I miss them so much."

"I miss them, too. Very much."

"I miss the way Mom would braid my hair every morning. And the way she made her eggs. She used to worry that she loved on us too much … too many hugs and kisses, but I liked that she did that. I loved all of her hugs … and now I miss them more than ever. I miss everything about her. I even miss the way she smelled."

"I miss her, too. I miss her smile, and the way she was always singing in the car. And her laugh … she was always so happy. And Daddy, too. He was so goofy sometimes. I remember the year we went to Florida for summer vacation. It was such a long drive, and when we finally got there, he got out of the car and started dancing in the middle of the road. I thought I would die of embarrassment at the time, but now … I'd give anything to have him dancing in the road again," I told her as tears started to trickle down my cheek.

"It's just not fair. I want them back. I want my momma and daddy back," she cried.

"I know you do. We all do. It's just hard right now, but it won't be like this forever, Hadley. The police are working hard, and when they catch the guys that hurt Mom and Dad, we'll go back home. You'll get to see your friends again, and …"

"No. I don't want to go back home," she cut me off. "Ever."

Her reaction surprised me. I thought she'd be eager

to get back home. "Why not?"

"I don't want to go back there if Mom and Dad aren't going to be there. It wouldn't be the same, and it'd make me miss them even more," she sniffled. "When things are safe again, maybe we can stay here or move somewhere else. I don't care. I just don't want to go back there."

"Okay … we'll figure it out. For now, you need to get some sleep. Do you want me to go lay down with you in your room?" I offered.

She tossed the covers back and sat up as she said, "No, that's okay. I'm feeling a little better now."

"Okay. I'm here if you need me."

I pulled the covers back over me and tried to fall back asleep, but it was useless. Mom and Dad were on my mind, and I couldn't stop wondering if the police had come up with any leads on their case. After tossing our cell phones, I'd called to give the lead detective my new number, but he hadn't called in weeks. I was beginning to think they'd never find the men who killed my parents, and the kids and I would be on the run forever. I couldn't let that happen. I needed to get in touch with him and push him to work harder so we could start to find some normalcy in our lives.

I eventually found sleep, but it wasn't enough. I woke up with tired eyes and a throbbing headache. I still had a few minutes before I needed to get the kids up, so I headed into the kitchen and started a pot of coffee. I'd just finished filling the pot with water when I heard my neighbor tapping lightly on the wall. When it stopped, I stood there staring at the blank wall in front of me and wondered what the hell he was doing. When he knocked a second time, I said, "What?"

He shouted back, "You want a shower?"

"What?" I'd heard what he'd said, but my brain wasn't quite awake and I didn't know what else to say.

"Do you want to use my shower," he asked louder than before.

A hot shower sounded wonderful, just what I needed to wake me up after a long night, but I was hesitant about going next door to use a stranger's bathroom.

When I didn't answer, he continued. "I'm about to leave, so you'll have the place to yourself."

The offer was too good to refuse, so I shouted, "Yes! I'll be right over."

I quickly gathered a change of clothes and a clean towel and headed out into the hallway. I hadn't even had time to knock when his door flew open. He was wearing his leather jacket with a pair of worn blue jeans and boots, and even with his shaggy hair falling down around his brow, I could still see those gorgeous green eyes staring back at me. With a friendly smile, he motioned for me to come inside. "I'm headed out. Just lock up when you leave."

I stepped inside. I didn't even have time to thank him before the door shut behind me. With him gone, I took a moment to glance around his apartment, and I was astounded at how nice his place was compared to ours. It was freshly painted, and it even had a few pictures hanging on the wall. It smelled so clean, and the furniture didn't look like it had come from some secondhand store. I stepped into the kitchen and saw that he even had a washer and dryer. It was hard not to be a little jealous, but as soon as I stepped into that hot shower, all of my negative thoughts started to slip away. I was able to let my worries go and just enjoy the warmth of the water against my skin. Unfortunately, the clock was ticking, so my moment of peace and quiet didn't last long. Once I was dressed, I quickly cleaned up my mess and, after locking his front door, I headed back to my apartment. To my surprise, the kids were already up and getting dressed, giving me a few extra minutes to finish up my morning routine.

Once Charlie and Hadley finished getting ready, they followed me downstairs. Charlie started out back to meet up with Louise, but before Hadley followed, she came over to me and said, "You look really pretty today."

"Thanks, squirt. That was sweet of you." I smiled and gave her a quick hug.

Her eyebrows furrowed into a serious look when she said, "And I didn't think you sounded like a hyena when you were screaming last night."

I shook my head and groaned, "Oh, sweetie. Don't even give it a second thought. Let's just forget any of that ever happened."

"Okay," she smiled and rushed out back to meet up with her brother.

Once they were both gone, I started my shift and didn't stop until my afternoon break. I decided to use the time to call Detective Brakeman to see if there had been any changes in the case. I'd bought a cheap phone with a pay as you go plan, hoping that no one would be able to trace my calls. I grabbed it out of my purse and headed out into the alley to dial his number. It took me several tries, but I finally managed to get him to answer.

"It's good to hear from you, Olivia. How is Memphis treating you?" he asked in a much too friendly tone.

"Memphis is great. There's never a dull moment," I said with a dry laugh. "I had a few minutes, so I thought I'd check with you to see if you'd had any leads on the case."

He covered the phone while he cleared his throat, then said, "There's been a few things that have come to our attention over the last couple of days, Olivia. Maybe you should come in so we can discuss what we've found."

"I'm over twenty hours away, Detective. If there is something you need to tell me, then tell me," I pushed.

"Your father's business partner, Mr. Perry, committed suicide last week. Upon further investigation, we discovered that he might have been involved with your father's murder."

"Mr. Perry? No … that isn't possible. Mr. Perry

loved my parents. He'd never do anything to harm them!" When my father started his real estate company, Mr. Perry was the first person he hired. Over the years, they'd become close friends. We were always doing things with their family, like weekend cookouts, and we even vacationed together. When we were younger, his son Daniel and I were close, but things changed as we got older. His dad sent him away to some prep school for boys, and after that, he wasn't around as much. We were all like family. There's no way Mr. Perry was involved.

"I'm afraid the evidence says otherwise, but the investigation is still underway. There are several leads we are looking into, so it's just a matter of time before we find out who is responsible. Just hang tight and let us do our jobs."

"Yeah, well, that's easier said than done," I groaned.

"How so? Have you run into any trouble since you left?"

"No. We haven't had any of that kind of trouble. So far, I haven't noticed anyone following us or even looking for us. Hopefully it will stay that way."

"If anything changes, call me."

"Thanks, Detective Brakeman. If something changes, you'll be the first to know. I'll be in touch soon to see if you found out anything more about Mr. Perry."

"Stay safe, Olivia," he commanded before hanging

up the phone.

Knowing I only had a few minutes left of my break, I stayed outside and took a minute to myself to think. I tried to remember my father's partnership with Mr. Perry and how they worked together—the good *and* the bad—but no red flags came to my mind. My father had trusted him. So did the rest of my family, and just the thought of him being involved with my parents' murder sent chills down my spine. As desperate as I was to find out who had been responsible for my parents' death, I prayed that we all hadn't been wrong about Mr. Perry.

Chapter 6
Clutch

While most people were just getting up to pour their morning's first cup of coffee, I was on my bike and on my way to the warehouse. It was colder than I'd expected and the chill in the air clung to me like a wet blanket. Ignoring my freezing balls, I followed Gus's directions to the clubhouse. As I pulled up to the gate, one of the prospects came rushing towards me, but as soon as he noticed my Satan's Fury patch, he stopped and motioned me through. I pulled my bike up front, and after I parked, I went inside to look for Gus.

I hadn't gotten far when Lowball, one of the brothers, approached me. He was young, maybe in his early twenties, but he was a big dude with broad round shoulders like a linebacker and was covered from head to toe with tattoos and piercings. When I told him why I was there, he led me down a long hall to Gus's office. He knocked, and once Gus answered, Lowball opened the door, letting me know it was okay to step inside.

When I entered the small room, Gus, a muscled-up older man with a long full beard, was sitting behind his desk. He was talking a mile a minute on his cellphone, and without stopping his conversation, he greeted me with a quick chin-lift and then nodded his head towards the chair in front of him. By the time I'd taken my seat, he was off the phone and said, "So, you're the Clutch that Cotton has been telling me about. You know, I expected you to be *bigger*."

I was six-three and two-forty. I laughed and said, "Yeah, well ... I've missed a few meals while I was out on the road."

"Glad you made it here alright. Was the apartment okay? You need anything over there?"

"Nah, it's all good. The place is just right. I appreciate you putting me up."

Gus was in his late sixties, older than most in his rank, but it was obvious by his thick, burly build that the man was still holding his own. He was tough. There was a hardness behind his eyes, and anyone could see that he'd be one to reckon with if there was ever any trouble with the club. As president of the Memphis Chapter, he'd have to be harder and smarter than most. The gang problem in the area was no secret, so not only did they have issues with localized competition, they also had to deal with the cops. With all the crime in the area, someone was always watching, and it only took one slip to fuck everything up. The smile dropped from his face as he leaned forward and said, "You got something to show me?"

I reached into my jacket pocket and said, "Yeah, I

got it." I pulled out the map, and, as soon as I started to unroll it, he got busy clearing off his desk. Once he was done, I laid it out before him. "It'll involve four of our club chapters: Salt Lake, Denver, Topeka, and Oklahoma City."

His shoulders relaxed a bit and he eased back in his chair. He crossed his arms and began nodding in approval. "Good strong chapters. Shouldn't be any problems working with them."

"Agreed. They'll do their part to make sure everything goes as planned. To get things rolling, our club will pick up our part of the delivery at Port Angeles and get it down to the brothers at Salt Lake. Then, they'll add to it and get it to Denver, and so on, until everything gets down here to you."

"We'll be ready. I've got us barge access lined up, so we won't have any problem getting the shipment down to Baton Rouge. As long as that river doesn't flood, we're covered."

"Good deal. I'll let Cotton know. He said you needed a hand in the garage while I was here."

"My lead mechanic got pretty mangled when his bike got away from him. He was on his way home when he hit a curve covered with loose sand. With all the rain we've been having, he should've known better. Now the garage is backed up."

"I'll do what I can to help you out," I offered.

"Much appreciated. Cotton said that you were one of the best."

"Yeah. I know my way around an engine, especially the classics," I added with a smile.

He stood and started for the door. "Then you should be as happy as a pig in shit when you see the garage. I'll have one of the boys take you over." I nodded and followed him down the hall to the back door. After talking to one of the prospects, he came back over to me and held out his hand. "Crow is gonna take you over to the garage. Just follow him. And remember… call me if you need anything."

I shook his hand. "Will do, Boss."

After the prospect got on his bike, I followed him over to the club's garage. It was just a few blocks from the diner, and there was a huge blue sign with the name Lou's Restorations hanging just beneath the roof. It wasn't a new shop, but it was in decent condition. Crow parked his bike and led me inside to meet Blaze, the guy in charge of the garage until their lead guy got back on his feet. When he saw us approaching, a curious look crossed his face and I could see that he was sizing me up, questioning if I was there to take over his job. He wasn't a small guy, but like most, he was several inches shorter than me. With his blonde hair and unruly beard, he reminded me of that guy from that chick flick—I think it was called *The Notebook* or something. I should've been able to remember the guy's name. Cass made me watch that shit four or five times, and after seeing Blaze, my mind went straight to them out in that boat around all those damn swans.

He pulled me from my thoughts when he asked, "You Clutch?"

"That'd be me," I answered. "Guess you're the man in charge."

"Yeah, that'd be me … at least for now," he answered. "Duggar will be back in a couple of weeks."

"Gus sent me over to see if I could help out, maybe get y'all caught back up. Where do you want me to start?" I asked, even though I'd do what I'd always done. First, I'd do a thorough inspection of each car, going over the entire vehicle one section at a time. Then, I'd take stock of the condition of all the body parts—interior, electrical, engine, exhaust, suspension, and frame. Once I had a list of what needed to be done, then I'd get to work.

"Dive right in, brother. We've got three in the main garage, and there are two more out back. And we'll have another one coming in later today," Blaze explained. "I'll be working in the back on the Chevy if you need anything."

He started towards the rear of the garage, and for the first time, I realized there was only one other mechanic working. I called out to him and asked, "Hey, where is everybody?"

"You're looking at it, brother … at least for today. I have a couple of guys that will be coming in tomorrow."

"What the hell? Two guys running the entire garage?"

"Yeah … it sucks. Right now, the garage makes the

least amount of money, so we get the least amount of help. A good bit of the body detailing, sandblasting and chrome, is sent out. All interior work is done around the corner at Lenny's Upholstery."

"Fuck."

"Yep."

Hell. No wonder they were so fucking behind. There wasn't much I could do about it, so I shook it off and said, "Guess I'll get started."

Without even stopping for a lunch break, I spent the next seven hours working my ass off in the garage. I'd dismantled the first engine and would have gotten more done, but I couldn't get Hazel out of my head. The longer I worked, the more distracted I became with images of her in that wet t-shirt. I decided to call it a day, convincing myself that I had to leave early so I could make a stop at the hardware store before it closed. I wanted to get that shower fixed before Hazel got off work, hoping that I wouldn't spend another day tormented with thoughts of the mysterious brunette.

Before leaving, I grabbed a few tools and headed over to Blaze. He'd already finished up with the Chevy and was working in the office when I walked up. I tapped on the glass window and said, "Calling it a day. I borrowed a few tools for the night. Have a little project to work on back at the apartment.

"No problem."

"I'll be back in the morning."

He looked up at me and, with sincerity in his voice,

he said, "Appreciated your help today."

"Anytime," I told him as I went to the side door and walked over to my bike. I made a stop at the hardware store around the block and gathered up everything I needed to fix the shower. I quickly realized that I couldn't carry everything I needed on my bike. Thankfully, the kid behind the counter offered to deliver it since he was on his way home. I helped him load everything into the bed of his truck and led him back to the apartment.

Once he was parked, he rolled down his window and asked, "You want a hand getting it all inside?"

"Nah, I got it." Once I'd gotten everything out of the back of the truck, I closed the tailgate and walked over to the driver's side window and handed him a twenty. "Thanks, man."

He tipped his hat as he put the truck in reverse and pulled out of the lot. It was cumbersome with the sheet of drywall and all my tools, but I managed to get everything up the stairs in one trip. My hands were full, so I used the tip of my boot to knock on the door.

Moments later, David poked his head out of the door. When he saw all the stuff in my hands, he asked, "You really gonna fix that piece of crap shower?"

"That's the plan," I answered as I stepped into the apartment. "Your sister still at work?"

"Yeah. She won't be home for another hour or so."

I started down the hallway, feeling relieved that I could get a good start on fixing everything before she got back. "Good. I should have most of it done before then."

"You need a hand?" he offered as he reached for the sheet of drywall.

"Thanks, bud."

Once we had everything laid out in the bathroom, he looked over to me and said, "You know, I don't even know your name."

Thinking back, I realized he was right. I smiled and said, "You can call me Clutch."

His eyes skirted to the ground for a brief second, like he was mulling over what he was about to say next. Then he looked back over to me and said, "I guess you can call me David. My sister's name is Cindy."

"David, it is. Can you pass me the wrench?"

As he reached into the toolbox, he asked, "You're in a motorcycle club, right? So, Clutch is like your road name or something?"

"Yeah, I picked it up when I was working at our garage back home. My real name is Thomas, but no one really calls me that anymore."

"I think it'd be cool to be in a club like that," he told me as he handed me the wrench.

"It has its moments."

We continued to talk back and forth as I disassembled the broken faucet and all the broken plumbing. In no time, we had the new showerhead installed and a new nozzle on the faucet. There was still a hole in the drywall, but I was running out of time.

They'd still be able to take a shower, so I decided to leave that for the following day.

Once I had my mess cleaned up and all my tools back in my bag, David asked, "You want a drink or something? I think we've got some sweet tea made up."

Knowing Hazel would be home any minute, I told him, "Nah, I gotta get going. I'll be back tomorrow to finish up the drywall and paint."

"You're gonna paint it, too?"

"Yeah, it could use a fresh coat … maybe two." Honestly, the entire apartment could use a coat of paint and some other basic updates to make it more like mine. As I was walking out into the hall, the little sister popped out of her room, blocking my path. I smiled and said, "Hey there, beautiful."

A light blush crossed her face when she said, "Hi… I … just wanted to say thanks for fixing our shower."

"No problem, sweetheart. Glad to do it."

She was twirling a long strand of her hair around her finger as she took a step closer to me and softly said, "Just so you know … I think you hurt Sis's feelings last night when you called her a dying hyena."

"Whoa … wait a minute. I never actually called her a hyena. I just said she sounded like one when she was doing all that screaming last night."

"It wasn't very nice."

"No … I guess it wasn't," I admitted. For a kid her age, she was doing a pretty good job of busting my balls for being an ass. "I guess I should probably apologize for that."

"Maybe, but don't do it because of me. You should do it because you want to, not because I said something about it."

Damn. She sounded just like my mother—and even looked like her as she stood there with her hand on her hip and a stern look on her face.

I nodded and cleared my throat. "Got it."

"Thanks again for fixing our shower," she told me as she stepped back into her room and shut the door.

"Check you later, dude," I told David before walking out of the apartment. It was getting late and I still hadn't had anything to eat. I figured I had just enough time to make it down to the diner for one of those famous cheeseburgers and maybe, if the mood strikes, a good old-fashioned apology.

Chapter 7
Olivia

"I was enlisted for over twenty years. Would've stayed longer if I hadn't blown out my knee. It was the best time of my life, but I tell ya … lots of things changed since the day I first joined," Sam told me as he took another bite of his fries. He'd started talking as soon as I sat down in the booth in front of him to wrap napkins around the silverware. Even from several feet away, I could see a glint of happiness when he talked about that particular time in his life.

Hoping he'd keep talking, I asked, "What kind of changes?"

"Ah, nothing that really mattered. Back when I first enlisted, the boys could wear beards, long and burly. No one cared much," he answered. After taking another bite of his burger, he said, "And back then it took months for us to get mail. It was well past Easter before we got our Christmas cards, but satellites and computers changed all that."

"That had to be hard. I'm too impatient for that." I smiled.

"I don't know. I think we appreciated it a lot more back then. Now everything comes too easy, if you know what I mean."

"Yeah, that makes sense."

"You remember when the Challenger went down in '86?"

"The Space Shuttle? The one with the teacher onboard?"

"Yeah. I was there when it happened. We were called out to help recover the debris. They had helicopters and our guys out in boats searching for days, but we never found much. We all knew we wouldn't, but we kept at it."

"It was a bit before my time, but I remember my teacher getting really upset whenever she showed us the video. It was so sad."

"I don't think I'll ever forget that day … how the cloud of smoke just hung in the air for hours."

Once I'd finished working on the silverware, I looked over at the clock and was relieved to see that I only had fifteen more minutes left of my shift. I got up and said, "I hate to cut you short, but I have to finish up a few things before I leave. Can I get you anything else?"

"No, dear. I'm fine. You go do what you gotta do."

I grabbed the box of silverware and headed to the back to put them away, but when I turned the corner, I noticed that my mysterious, too-hot-for-his-own-good new neighbor was sitting in my section. I had no idea how long he'd been sitting there, so with my hands still full, I walked over to him. "Hey. Can I get you something?"

With a coy smile, he looked up at me. "I'll take a sweet tea and a burger with onion rings."

That smile caught me off-guard. Those lips curled into a sexy smirk, the scruff of his day-old beard, the hint of mischief that lurked behind those beautiful green eyes … it all had me going into sensory overload. I needed to respond. I needed to say something, but I just stood there, locked in my own prison of thoughts as I stared at his mouth. What was it about this man that had me acting like such a fool? And why did those damn lips make me want to bite my own? I finally pulled myself out of my lust-induced fog and said, "I'll be right back with your sweet tea."

"Thanks, Hazel," he purred, making the hairs on the back of my neck prickle against my skin, which made me want to kick myself. He hadn't even called me by my real name and I was getting all worked up. As much as I hated to admit it, the man had an effect on me, and it was getting harder and harder to ignore. I wanted to think that my attraction towards him was just because he was hot. I wanted to believe that it would pass, but the more I was around him, I realized that it was so much more than his looks that drew me to him. Confidence radiated off of him, shining like a new dime, and I felt like a moth being pulled into the light.

I took a minute to shake off the effects of his

charms, and when I returned with his glass of iced tea, I said, "Thanks for the help last night … and letting me use your shower this morning. I really appreciated it."

"No problem. And about last night, I wanted to apologize for that hyena comment. You didn't actually sound like a *dying hyena,*" he said with a chuckle. He paused for a brief moment. There was a little spark of mischief that crossed his eyes before he added, "It was more like the sound you get when you stomp on a cat's tail."

"Really? And that's supposed to be better? I did not sound like a dying hyena or a cat!" I growled.

"Oh, come on. Don't be so uptight," he teased. The corners of his mouth curled into a sexy grin, making his criticism sting even more. "I was just messin' around."

As soon as the word uptight rolled from his lips, my blood began to boil. I had to swallow all of the profanities that came rushing through my head and instead forced the words, "Do me a favor. Save your 'messin' around' for someone else." Like an idiot, I brought my hands up and used my fingers to make imaginary quotation marks when I said "messin' around".

I immediately regretted my little hand gesture, when he did the same to me as he teased, "I don't know, Hazel. I think a little *'messin' around'* might be just what you need to loosen you up."

I didn't miss the sexual undertone of his little comment, so I snapped, "And I bet you think you're just the guy for this messin' around."

An intensity I hadn't expected crossed his face when he replied, "No doubt about that."

"Whatever."

Before he had a chance to make another smart-ass comment, I quickly turned and headed back into the kitchen before I said something I would regret. He had ties with Louise, and the last thing I needed to do was piss him off and risk losing my job.

I decided right then and there that I was done dealing with him. I could not afford to care that just the sight of him turned me into a horny teenager. I was over it. A man like that just wasn't worth the frustration or the risk. When Cyrus placed his order in the window, I decided to save myself the hassle of trying to deal with Mr. Obnoxious and asked Ashton, one of the other waitresses, to deliver the plate to him. Then I clocked out and headed upstairs.

When I walked into the apartment, Charlie and Hadley were piled up on the sofa eating chips and watching some cop show on the TV. I took a step closer and was surprised to see that they both had wet heads. I sat down next to Hadley and, after inhaling the scent of soap, I knew they'd just taken a shower.

Noticing the surprised look on my face, Charlie said, "Clutch came and fixed the shower today."

"Clutch?"

"Yeah. You know, the guy from next door," he clarified. "He came after school and brought all this stuff to fix the shower. He didn't finish, so he's coming back tomorrow to fix that big old hole in the wall and to paint."

Guilt washed over me, hitting me in waves, as I thought about all the trouble he must have gone through to fix that stupid shower. Even though he'd told me that he'd fix it, I never believed that he'd actually do it. Why did he have to go and do something so freaking nice? It was so much easier to just think he was a complete asshole.

"Well, crap," I mumbled.

"What's wrong?" Hadley asked.

"I think I messed up," I admitted. "I may have been wrong about this Clutch guy." I'd made a real mess of things. I'd let my attraction towards him cloud my thinking, and instead of realizing that he was just joking around, I took his silly comments as an insult, letting it hurt my feelings and making me act like a complete jerk. Thinking back, he'd been nothing but nice all along, and I'd been hateful and rude. He had to think I was a complete bitch.

"He seems really nice, Livie. He did all that work in the bathroom, then cleaned up his mess and everything. And before he left, he said he was going to apologize for calling you a hyena. I think he felt a little bad about that. Did he apologize to you?"

"Yeah, sweetie. He did, but his apology needed a little work." I laughed. "I didn't know he'd fixed the shower, and I might have acted a bit rude to him. I guess

I'm the one that needs to do some apologizing now. And I'll have to do something to thank him for fixing the shower."

Hadley perked up and squealed, "Oh, I know! We could make him one of mom's chocolate cakes!"

I thought about it for a second, then answered, "Yeah, I think that would be perfect."

It was time for a little redemption, and even though I wasn't exactly trying to win Clutch's heart—at least not yet—I'd always heard that the way to win a man over was through his stomach. I had no doubt Mom's chocolate cake would be impossible for him to resist, and hopefully just what I needed to get him to accept my apology … if I wasn't too late.

Chapter 8
Clutch

Whatever pull I felt towards the hot little brunette who lived next door was gone. I was over it. Not that it had ever really even begun. She'd been nothing but a pain in the ass since the first day I'd laid eyes on her, and I'd given up all hope that she'd ever show me that softer side of herself that she showed everyone else. I'd seen how good she was with the kids and how she was always so friendly to her customers—even the homeless guy that she'd fed out of her own tips ... twice. I had no idea why she'd chosen to spit nothing but venom out at me, but I was done. I no longer gave a flying fuck how she looked at me with those gorgeous eyes, or the way her fingers trembled ever so slightly whenever she noticed that I was close to her. I didn't care that she was all I'd thought about since the moment I'd first laid eyes on her, that she'd completely captivated me with just one look. None of it mattered. Besides, the girl reeked of trouble. I had no idea what was going on with her, but I had no doubt she was hiding something. Something scared her enough to lie about who she was and give up the fancy-free life she used to have. It was plain to see, from the way that she talked to the way that she carried herself, that she'd come from good people—people with money and connections. She had no business working at Daisy Mae's diner much less living in that piece of shit apartment next door. All of it was fucking irrelevant. I was over it.

I was just about to call it a night when my burner started ringing. When I answered, Smokey shouted, "What's up, brother?"

His words were a little slurred, and I could hear the jukebox blaring in the background, letting me know that he was somewhere partying, so I asked him, "Where you at, Smoke?"

"At the clubhouse. A few of us are taking a break. Blowing off some steam after a long ass fucking day. Thought I'd call and check in on you."

"I'm good, Smoke."

"Good, good, good," he mumbled. "Maybe you will get your ass back home soon."

"It won't be much longer. Got a few things to finish up here and then I'll be on my way back," I assured him.

"Hey, Cass ... I need another beer," he shouted. For the first time in months, I didn't feel the punch in my gut from the sound of her name or the thought of her standing behind that bar ... or imagining the curves of her lips when she smiled. Nothing. The time away had done me good, but I knew the real reason for my change when Smoke asked, "You breaking any hearts down there?"

She was the first thing that came to my mind—my beautiful, fire-mouthed neighbor who had haunted my every thought since the moment I laid eyes on her. With her on my mind, I replied, "Only thing breaking around here is my fucking balls. This chick next door is giving me all kinds of hell."

"Ah, man. What are you complaining about?" He laughed. "There's nothing better than a hot little piece living next door."

"It's not like that, Smoke. This girl is a piece of work, and she has her brother and sister living with her. I've got a feeling that they're hiding from something, but she's keeping her shit guarded, brother. No way she's going to let me in."

"Sounds like you've got yourself a challenge there, Clutch. I'm sure it's nothing you can't handle," he heckled.

When I heard a woman's voice in the background saying "Come on, Smokey. It's time to play." I said, "Look man, I gotta run. Need to be at the garage early tomorrow."

"Don't work too hard, man. You gotta have a little fun, too. You know? I'll be in touch, soon," he told me as he hung up the phone.

I tossed my phone onto the table next to the bed and fell back, resting my head on my pillow. The room was dark and completely quiet except for the low muffled sounds of Hazel's voice coming through the walls. When I eased myself a little closer, I could barely make out the melody of a familiar song. It was one of those that my mother used to sing to me when I was having trouble sleeping. I closed my eyes, and with the calming sound of Hazel's voice floating in the air, I couldn't help but fall asleep.

The sun was barely streaming through the window blinds when I heard a loud bang against the wall of my bedroom. I was still rubbing the sleep from my eyes when I heard David shout, "Damn! Louise is going to leave us! We're already ten minutes late!"

"Maybe she waited," Hazel shouted back. "Just hurry up. Maybe we can still catch her. I'll go downstairs and tell her that you're coming."

Seconds later, I heard her front door slam followed by her footsteps clomping down the steps. David continued to slam things around his room. I got up and threw some clothes on, deciding that I might as well get up and going. I was about to leave when I heard the kids rush out of the apartment and slam the door behind them. While I was locking my door, I could hear David talking to Hazel at the end of the stairs.

"Your shift already started. Louise will crawl all over you if you take off just to take us to school. We'll just walk or take the stupid bus. It isn't a big deal."

Hazel's voice was strained with worry when she said, "No. It's just too risky. I'll just take you. It won't take long. Maybe Louise won't notice …"

I'd had about all of the fussing back and forth that I could take, so as I started down the steps, I announced, "I'll take them."

When I got to the bottom of the steps, they all stood there staring at me until David said, "Cool. That'll work."

"Umm ... no. I couldn't ask you to do that," Hazel protested.

"You didn't ask, but I'm offering. Just gonna need the keys to your car."

"Are you sure about this?" Hazel asked.

"Yeah, I'm sure." I held out my hand. As soon as she placed the keys in my palm, I shouted, "Load 'em up, guys. We gotta roll."

The kids rushed out the back door. I was just about to follow behind them when Hazel called, "Clutch?"

"Yeah?"

When I turned to face her, she gave me a sweet smile and, with her eyes full of warmth, she said, "Thank you."

And there it was. She'd finally shown me a glimpse of that softer side she'd shared with everyone else, and I wanted nothing more than to hold onto that moment for just a bit longer. Unfortunately, time was not on my side. The kids were waiting for me outside, so I said, "Anytime."

By the time I'd gotten the kids to school and returned the car, it was almost eight. I headed straight to the garage, and when I got there, several of the guys were already there and working. After I'd returned the tools I'd borrowed the day before, I went back over to the Ford I was trying to get finished and set to work. I'd been at it for almost an hour when I heard Blaze talking at the front gate. I stuck my head out from under the hood of the car and saw him standing next to a young woman, maybe in her early twenties, and she had a little boy with her. After a few seconds, Blaze reached down and took the boy in his arms, then placed the palm of his hand on the child's forehead. The girl turned to leave as they started walking towards the main office.

I went back to work, but it wasn't long before my attention was diverted from the engine to the little boy who was standing next to me. When I looked down at him, it was like seeing a mini version of Blaze with his sandy blonde hair and big brown eyes, leaving no doubt that it was his kid. He lifted up on his toes as he tried to get a peek under the hood, and when he couldn't get a good look, he turned to me and asked, "Whatcha doin'?"

"I'm working. What are you doing, little man?"

"I'm waiting on daddy to get off da phone … but he talks a lot. I think it's gonna be a while," he explained. He started to cough a little, then sniffed. "I got a fever so he's called my Gammy to come get me." Before I could get a word in, he asked, "What's your name? I haven't seen you here before."

"My name's Clutch. How about you? You got a name?" He was a cute kid, maybe six or seven, but he talked like he was much older.

He wiped his runny nose with the back of his hand as he scanned the body of the old Ford. "My name is Kevin, but everyone calls me Mini since I look so much like my dad. My Gammy says I look like my momma, but …"

"Kevin!" Blaze shouted.

"I'm over here wit' Clutch," he answered.

Blaze walked over. "Sorry, man. Been one of those days."

"No problem. I was enjoying the company," I told him.

Blaze looked over to Kevin. "Your grandmother will be here in a minute. She's gonna run you up to the clinic."

"Aw, man! Do I have to go to the stupid doctor?" he whined.

"Sorry, little buddy, but you do. It might just be a cold, but you know we can't take chances with those fevers," Blaze responded. "It's always better to be safe than sorry."

"Can't you take me? I don't want to go with Gammy. She always gets nervous and stuff."

"I can't today. I'm too far behind. We even brought in extra help. That's why Clutch is here."

"If you want to take him, I'll cover you. Don't mind staying late," I offered.

"Please, daddy," Kevin pleaded.

"I'll go with you to the doctor, but when we're

done, you're going home with your grandmother."

"I can do that." Kevin grinned. "Thanks, Clutch."

"No problem, little man. Good luck at the doctor's."

On their way out the door, Blaze turned back to me and said, "I should be back in about an hour. Call me if you need anything. Lowball has my number."

I spent the next few hours finishing up on the Ford's engine, and once I had it up and running, I headed over to Blaze's Chevy. He'd been working on the carburetor, so I finished the disassembly and was just about done cleaning it when Blaze walked back into the garage. The minute he hit the doorway, I could see that something was wrong. He came over to me and said, "I've got it from here. You can go on home if you want."

"Nah, I'm good for another hour. Is everything alright with Kevin?"

He let out a deep breath. "No … no it's not. He tested negative for the flu, and the doctor couldn't be sure why his fever was so high. There's a small chance that his cancer is back, so they are running some more tests. We won't know anything for sure until tomorrow."

"That's rough, man. How long has he been in remission?"

"Just over a year. He had a hard go of it. Spent almost a year in and out of St. Jude, but he finally beat it. I don't think I could take watching him go through all of that all over again." He ran his hand through his hair and sighed as he said, "He's been through so much already. Lost his mom a couple years back, and just when he was getting past it, we found out he had Leukemia."

"Fuck, man. I hate to hear that. If you don't mind me asking, what happened with his mother?"

"Car accident. She was hit by a drunk driver ... killed her instantly. She meant everything to me and losing her just about did me in, but having Kevin around got me through. Don't think I would've made it without him."

"Bet he'd say the same about you. It's good you've got each other, and if the cancer is back, it'll be tough, but you'll get through it. There's no other choice but to get through it, and you've got brothers who have your back when things go south."

"Been lucky there. Couldn't ask for more." He looked over at the old Ford and said, "Let's just call it a night. I'll come in early tomorrow and catch up."

"Sounds like a plan. I need to stop and grab some paint on my way home anyway. Need to get there before the hardware store closes."

"What kind of paint do you need?"

"Got a little project going on in my neighbor's bathroom."

With his eyebrow raised with suspicion, he smiled and asked, "What kind of project?"

"Man, you don't even want to know. Let's just say

that I'm helping out a damsel in distress," I chuckled.

"I bet you are!" He laughed. "We've got a couple of cans in the back from where Gus had the boys paint the office. Nothing fancy, but you're welcome to it."

"I think I'll take you up on that. Shouldn't take much."

"Take all you want, and there's paintbrushes and rollers back there, too," he let me know. "I'm heading out. Just lock up before you leave."

"Will do. Thanks, brother."

By the time I'd gotten everything strapped to my bike and back to the apartment, it was after six, which didn't give me much time to finish up the bathroom before Hazel got home. I hauled everything upstairs, and when I knocked on the door, Cindy shouted from the other side, "Who is it?"

"Clutch," I answered.

She opened the door with a huge smile on her face and said, "Hey. What's up?"

"Gonna finish the bathroom, but I'm going to need an assistant. You up for a little painting?"

"I'm not sure if I'd be any good at it, but I'll give it a shot," she offered.

"I don't think it could look any worse. Do you?" I asked as I headed down the hall.

"Guess not." She followed me. "Just tell me what you need me to do."

"Since the bathroom is small, we're gonna go on and paint all of it," I told her as I laid out a tarp on the floor. I opened the can of paint and handed her a brush as I said, "You start on that wall while I finish patching this hole."

"Is there a right way to do this?" she asked.

"Nope. Just go up and down with the brush until you cover the entire wall. That's about it."

She did a few strokes and then said, "This is so cool. Thanks for letting me help."

"Doing good. I knew you'd make a good assistant."

We hadn't been working long when David stuck his head in and said, "Hey. What's going on?"

"I'm helping Clutch paint. Doesn't it look good?" she asked proudly.

"Looks a lot better already. You need any help?"

"We got it," she insisted.

David ignored her and grabbed one of the extra brushes and started painting the spots that his sister couldn't reach. In just over an hour, the hole was patched and we'd finished painting the entire bathroom. The kids helped me clean up the mess, and I was long gone before Hazel got home from work. I was exhausted. My body ached everywhere and my head was pounding, so I skipped dinner and made myself comfortable on the sofa. I didn't even bother turning on the TV, choosing instead to listen to the comforting sounds of Hazel and the happy kids talking next door as I fell asleep.

Chapter 9
Olivia

"It looks great. I can't believe you helped him do all this," I told them as I stared at my new bathroom. With the fresh paint and fixtures, it didn't even look like the same room.

"I think Mom would have really liked it," Hadley whispered.

"Yeah, I think she would've been really impressed with all of your hard work," I agreed as I gave her a quick hug.

She looked up at me and asked, "Can we get a new shower curtain to match the new wall color?"

"That's a great idea. Maybe we can go look for one when you get out of school. I'm only working one shift tomorrow, so I'll be off early."

"Can we get some more cereal, too?" Charlie asked. "Hadley ate all the marshmallows out of the one I liked. Now all we have is the one with oats and raisins and it sucks."

"I did not eat all the marshmallows!"

"Yeah, you did. You always do. There's nothing

but dry cereal left and it's gross," Charlie complained.

"We'll get some more cereal. It's not the end of the world. We need to get some other groceries while we are out."

"We need to get the stuff to make Clutch's cake, too," Hadley reminded me. "Do you remember how to make it?"

"I think we can figure it out," I assured her. "I'll get us a list started, and as soon as I get off work, we'll go do some shopping. For now, I'm going to make us something for dinner. Have you both finished all of your homework?"

"All done," Hadley said proudly.

Charlie grumbled something under his breath, and then said, "I've got to finish up another paper for Mrs. Cole. She's such a pain. I don't think that woman likes anything. She's always giving everybody bad grades, and this paper we have to write is just stupid."

"Maybe I could help you with it," I offered. "What's it about?"

"I don't even know. Something about *The Scarlet Letter*. The book was okay, but she wants us to write from the woman's perspective or something stupid like that. I'm not some chick, so how am I supposed to write about her stinking perspective?"

"Yeah, I can definitely help with that one. I read that book in high school, too. You'll have to remind me of a few things, but I'm sure we can get it done. Let me fix something for us to eat, and then we'll knock it out."

"Cool. You want some help with dinner?"

"I've got it. I'm going to warm up some stew and make some grilled cheese sandwiches."

He started walking towards his bedroom and shouted, "I want two! I'm starving."

"You're always starving," I shouted back with a snicker.

After dinner, Charlie and I spent a couple of hours working on his paper, and by the time we were finished, I think it turned out pretty well. For someone who thought he knew nothing about the female's perspective, he had some pretty good insight where the book was concerned. Hadley was already sound asleep when I made my way to my spot on the sofa, and it didn't take long for me to join her in a deep slumber.

We woke up the next morning and hit the ground running. After work, we did our shopping, bought a few groceries and things for the house, finished laundry and homework, and then started on Clutch's cake. When I pulled it out of the oven, Hadley was tickled that it looked just like the ones mom used to make.

"Can I help with the icing?" she asked.

"Absolutely. You can do it all, but we need to wait for it to cool off first," I explained. The entire apartment smelled like chocolate heaven, and it was hard not to steal a taste for ourselves. "I think we're going to need to make another one, though."

"Why?" Hadley asked with a worried look.

"Look at it. Don't you want some?" I giggled.

"Let's make another one just for us."

"Really? That would be awesome!"

In no time, we had the second cake made, and Hadley was ready to start decorating the first. She was so cute sitting there trying her best to be precise and make the cake look perfect. She spent almost an hour making sure it was just right, and once she was done, she looked over to me and asked, "How does it look?"

I walked over to her, and as I looked at the beautiful creation, I said, "It looks amazing, Hadley. Clutch is going to love it."

"I hope so. He's been really nice, and I really want him to like it."

"Of course he's going to like it, sweetheart. It's mom's special recipe we're talking about here. He'd have to be crazy not to love it."

"Can we take it over to him now?"

"I don't know. It's getting a little late. I'd hate to wake him up. Maybe we can give it to him tomorrow," I suggested.

"But it's fresh now!"

"Okay." I gave in to those big pleading eyes of hers. I did my best to wrap it up without smearing the icing, then said, "Let's go see if he's home."

"I'll carry it," she insisted as she lifted it up off the counter. She was beaming with pride as we walked towards his door. Once I'd knocked, I looked over to her and thought she'd come unglued with impatience as we waited for him to answer the door.

Clutch

He didn't answer, so I knocked again. Finally, I heard him rustling around, and seconds later the door eased open. Clutch stood there with his hand propped against the doorframe wearing only a pair of basketball shorts. We were not greeted by the irritatingly playful neighbor we'd recently become accustomed to, but instead were faced with what looked like a ghost of the man we'd come to know. He was in a sad state. I was immediately concerned when I saw that all the color had completely drained from his face. There were dark circles under his eyes and tiny beads of sweat covering his brow, and I could see that he was having a hard time even standing. He looked over to me and tried to speak, but a strangled cough stole his words.

When he continued to hack and groan, I turned to Hadley and said, "Go back to the apartment."

Even though I knew she and Charlie had been given their flu shots, I didn't want to take any chances. With a disgruntled look, Hadley placed the cake in my hands and asked, "Is he going to be okay?"

"He'll be fine," I assured her. Once she was gone, I turned back to Clutch and said, "You look like shit."

"I feel like shit," he answered with his voice strained and hoarse. "Don't know what the hell is wrong."

"We need to get you back in the bed." I walked past him and placed the cake down on the table before returning. I slipped my hand around his elbow, giving him a slight tug as I led him across the living room and into his bedroom. Realizing for the first time just how big he really was, I said, "You're tall."

"No. You're just short." He tried to laugh but just ended up coughing.

"I'm almost five-ten. That's not short," I corrected him. When we reached the edge of his bed, I pulled back the covers and said, "Get in."

"Bossy little thing, aren't ya," he mumbled as he crawled into the bed. The muscles in his arms and legs began to tremble as he reached for the covers, and after he pulled the blankets up to his chin, he whined, "It's freezing in here."

"It's not cold." I placed the palm of my hand on his forehead and said, "You're burning up. We really need to get you to a doctor."

"No, I just need some sleep," he argued, barely able to keep his eyes open. "Maybe some aspirin or something. My head is pounding and I hurt everywhere. I feel like I've been hit by a Mack truck."

"I'll get you something for the fever. It will help with the aches and pains," I told him as I walked out of the room. When I returned from my apartment a few minutes later with some Tylenol cold medicine, a bottle of Gatorade, and a cold rag, he'd already fallen asleep. He looked so sweet lying there, almost angelic, and I couldn't help but feel sorry for him. I knelt down beside him and gently nudged him until his eyes crept open. "You need to take this."

He lifted up on his elbow and took the medicine,

then fell back onto the bed, closing his eyes as I placed the cold rag on his head. He coughed again before saying, "Thanks, Hazel."

"I'm going to let you sleep. I'll be back a little later to check on you. I'm going to take your keys with me so I can get back in," I told him, but he wasn't listening. He'd already fallen back asleep.

When I got back to the apartment, the kids were getting ready for bed. I went in to check in on Hadley and she immediately asked, "How's Clutch?"

"He's pretty sick, but I think he'll be okay."

"He's all alone. Are you going to take care of him?" she asked.

"I'll do what I can, but Clutch is a big boy. I'm pretty sure he can take care of himself."

She shook her head. "Not when he's sick, Livie. Momma always said that men are at their worst when they're sick."

I smiled. "Well, she wasn't wrong about that, so I'll do what I can to help him."

Relief washed over her. "Good. He's going to need you. Maybe you could make him some of your chicken noodle soup."

"Maybe. Let's just wait and see how he's feeling tomorrow."

After the kids went to bed, I finished cleaning the kitchen and folded another load of laundry. By the time I was done, it was almost midnight. I stared at the wall, wondering if Clutch was doing any better, and finally decided that there was only one way to find out. I crept across the hall and tapped on his door. I didn't expect him to answer, but I figured it was the polite thing to do. I waited a few seconds, then used his key to open the door. I was a little apprehensive as I stepped inside his apartment. Even though I had a good reason for intruding, I still felt a bit uneasy about walking into a strange man's home without permission. Ignoring my anxiety, I tiptoed down the hall and into Clutch's bedroom. I turned on the light as I entered and found him sprawled out over the bed, legs on top of pillows, his head hanging off the side, and his mouth draped wide open. The covers had found their way to the floor and there was no sign of the cold rag I'd placed on his forehead. I stepped closer and put my hand on his forehead to check his fever again, and the minute my palm touched the heat of his skin, I panicked. He was hot, dangerously hot, so I rushed out of the room and headed over to my apartment for a thermometer.

When I returned, I placed my hand on his chest and pushed, trying to get him to wake up long enough for me to take his temperature. Finally, I got him to open his eyes and I said, "Open up. I need to see how high your fever is."

Thankfully, he didn't argue and let his mouth fall open. Once I'd placed the end of the thermometer under his tongue, he closed his mouth. While I waited for it to beep, I found the wet rag and placed it back on his forehead. When it was ready, I took the thermometer from his mouth and became immediately concerned when it read one hundred and three point five.

"Clutch," I whispered. "Your fever is really high. I think we should get you to the emergency room."

He rolled to his side and groaned, "No … tomorrow."

It was like dealing with a two-year-old. I nudged him again and said, "Yes."

He shook his head and growled, "*No*."

"Fine. But you need to take another dose of medicine and drink some fluids immediately. Your fever is dangerously high, and if the meds don't kick in, you're going to the emergency room, even if I have to call 911 to get you there!"

He started grumbling under his breath, but I ignored him and went into the kitchen to get the medicine I'd brought over earlier and poured him a glass of Gatorade. When I returned, his body was trembling again, making me worry even more. I sat down next to him on the edge of the bed and held the drink for him as he took his medicine. When he tried to lay back down, I said, "No way, mister. Sit up here and drink some more of this."

"I don't want it," he protested.

"I didn't ask you if you wanted it, Clutch. I said drink it. You need to get some fluids into your system." He bitched and moaned under his breath, but he continued to drink. When he emptied the glass, I told him, "That's more like it."

He looked up at me, and with puppy dog eyes and a

childlike expression, he said, "You're so pretty."

"You're delusional. It must be the fever," I teased. "Get some rest."

"I bought a lottery ticket," he announced.

Knowing he was just mumbling in his sleep, I grabbed his covers from the floor and draped them over him, then turned out the light and sat in the chair beside his bed. I didn't want to leave him until I knew his fever had gone down. It took almost forty-five minutes, but thankfully it dropped down to just a little over a hundred degrees. Even though his temperature had dropped, I was still worried about leaving him. After checking on him once more, I went back to my apartment and, before I went to sleep, I changed the time on my alarm to an hour earlier than I usually get up. I wanted to be sure I had plenty of time to check on Clutch before I had to get the kids to school and get to work. I finally made it over to the sofa and lay down. When I closed my eyes, Clutch's face was the first thing that popped into my mind. I kept seeing him say, "You're so pretty," over and over again.

Heaven help me. I was in trouble

Chapter 10
Clutch

I was in Hell. Pure, unadulterated Hell.

I felt like I'd been put through a meat grinder. Twice. I couldn't breathe. Every muscle in my body ached and my head felt like it was stuck in a vise grip, but that was only half of it. Instead of lying comfortably in my bed, I was sitting in some walk-in clinic downtown. The little ray of sunshine from next door wouldn't stop pestering me, going on and on about my stupid high fever and cough. I wanted to tell her to leave me the hell alone, but when I saw the worried look in her eyes, I finally agreed to go. So there I sat, surrounded by a bunch of sick folks wishing I was still in my bed. I could barely keep my fucking eyes open, but every time I tried to doze off, some kid would start screaming, making it impossible for me to go to sleep. I was miserable, and when I looked over at Hazel and saw that she seemed totally unaffected by the chaos around us, it only made me feel more irritated.

"Shouldn't you be at work or dealing with the kids or *something*?" I grumbled.

Without looking in my direction, she answered, "Yes, but Louise let me off."

I closed my eyes and rested my head on the wall behind me as I said, "Didn't take her for an easygoing boss. Figured she'd give you hell about missing a shift."

"When I told her that I was taking you to the doctor, she was actually really nice about it. Even said she wouldn't cut my pay for the day." There was a hint of surprise in her voice when she said, "Now that you mention it, she was *oddly nice* about it."

"I'll have to thank her the next time I see her," I told her sarcastically.

I felt her turn in her seat to face me. "Why was she so nice about it? Are you related to her or something?"

I opened my eyes and said, "Not exactly, but you could say we're family."

"How are you family if you're not related?" she pushed.

"That's how it works when you're a member of the club; you're family."

"Louise is a member of a motorcycle club?" she squealed. "No freaking way."

I was about to respond when another one of my coughing fits took over, forcing me to lean forward to catch my breath. I rested my elbows on my knees and was still gasping for air when Hazel ran her hand across my back, drawing my attention away from my lack of oxygen and over to the warmth of her touch. As I focused on the movement of her hand, my breathing quickly returned to normal, and to my surprise, she didn't take her hand away. Instead, she continued to rub my aching muscles and even ran her nails over my scalp, turning me into a big fucking puddle of mush. She'd gotten to me. She'd given me a little more of that softer side of hers, and I liked it.

But I wanted more … much, much more.

I could've sat there for hours letting her make imaginary trails across my head and back, but unfortunately a nurse called out my name, letting us know it was time to go back to see the doctor. Hazel quickly stood up and, once she'd helped me get to my feet, we followed the nurse to the back. Two hours later, we'd finally made it back to my apartment. Turns out Hazel was right about going to the doctor. I had the flu, and for the meds to work, I had to take it within the first twenty-four hours. I didn't miss the smile on her face when she brought the medicine over to me. Oh yeah; she was gloating. I chose to ignore Little Miss know-it-all and, after I swallowed the pills, I pulled the covers over me and closed my eyes.

"How about something to eat?"

"I'm not hungry," I mumbled.

"You need to try to eat something, Clutch. The label said to take it with food. I could go downstairs and get you some soup."

"No."

"How about a chocolate shake?"

I cracked one eye open, glaring at her as I growled,

"No."

"Whatever," she huffed. "Don't say I didn't try."

She walked out of the room, and seconds later I heard my front door slam. The room suddenly felt unbearably empty and quiet ... too fucking quiet, making me immediately regret acting like such an ass. I considered texting her with an apology, but quickly realized I had no way to get in touch with her. Fuck. I screwed up, and unfortunately at that moment there was nothing I could do about it. I rolled over and put the pillow over my head, trying to block out the guilty feeling that was gnawing at the pit of my stomach. I'd just about fallen asleep when I heard my door open and shut. Seconds later, Hazel appeared with a tray of food and a determined look on her face.

"What's all that?"

"Food. Now, sit up so you can eat something," she ordered. "No whining or complaining either."

I pulled myself up into a sitting position as I said, "I haven't whined."

"Oh yeah, you have. You're an old pro. I bet you drove your mother nuts with all your pouting," she teased.

"Stop picking on me. I'm sick. I might be actually dying over here."

"And dramatic, too. Bless her heart." She placed the tray on the bed next to me. "I don't know how she put up with you."

"It was easy. I was a good kid and pretty damn

good-looking, too."

With the tips of her fingers, she brushed the long strands of hair out of my face as she replied, "Maybe so, but I doubt it." She paused for a minute as she studied my face, then said, "You know … with all this hair, I think I'm going to start calling you Shaggy."

"No. Not gonna happen," I told her as I reached for the bowl of soup. "I've already got a name. Two, actually."

"Shaggy Thomas." She laughed. "That's two names."

"*Hazel*," I warned.

"I kind of like it. It has a nice ring to it." She got up and started for the kitchen as she said, "How about some more to drink, Shaggy?"

"How about I tan your hide if you call me Shaggy again?"

"Ha!" she called out from the kitchen. "Like you could tan anyone's hide in your sickly state."

"I'm not *that* sick."

She walked back into the room carrying a fresh drink and said, "Is that right? And to think a few minutes ago you thought you were dying."

"I may be sick, but I've got a good memory, Hazel. Just know, you've got one coming."

She rolled her eyes and smiled as she said, "I can't wait … *Shaggy*."

There was something about her smile that got to me. Maybe it was the spark in her eyes or just seeing the playful side of her. I don't know what it was, but I liked it. I liked it a lot. The more I was around her, the more I wanted to know about her. I wanted to know everything there was to know ... including whatever it was that she was hiding. I knew it was too soon, so I didn't push her to talk about it. I could be patient, and I had no doubt that she was worth the wait.

I finally managed to eat some of the homemade soup she'd brought, but by the time I was done, my body gave out on me. Without meaning to, I fell back to sleep. By the time I woke back up, the room was completely dark. I had no idea what time it was, but I didn't care. I still felt awful and was content to just lay there in the silence. The longer I laid there, the more I thought about the woman I'd come to know as Hazel. She was a mystery to me, a mystery I was determined to solve. She was hiding something. They all were—their names, where they were from, and what had driven them from their home. It must've been bad, otherwise a woman like her wouldn't be working in some diner and living in some shithole apartment. I had most of the pieces, but the missing ones were keeping me from putting the puzzle together. I wanted those missing pieces. I needed to know all there was to know about her.

I'd been lying there thinking for almost an hour when Hazel tapped on my bedroom door.

Seconds later, the lights came on and she stepped into the room carrying another tray of food. She smiled and asked, "Hey. You up for eating a little something?"

Her hair was down and she was wearing an oversized sweatshirt with a pair of cutoff shorts. I couldn't help but notice how sexy her legs looked in those damn shorts as she walked over to me. I eased myself up on the pillow and replied, "Yeah, I could eat."

"We had some leftover spaghetti, but if you're not up for that, I brought more soup, too."

"Spaghetti sounds good."

She sat the food down next to me and asked, "You feeling any better?"

"Well, I'm not dead, so I guess that's a plus," I chuckled.

"So dramatic," she giggled as she sat down at the foot of the bed. "I hate to break it to you, but I think you're going to live."

"I don't know. It's still pretty early," I teased. "I could always take a turn for the worse."

She lightly slapped my leg and said, "You are such a mess."

"I've been called worse."

"I can only imagine. Before I forget, I talked to Louise earlier. She thinks you might have caught the flu from some kid named Kevin?"

"Kevin? Are you sure? His dad said he tested negative."

"Well, he's got it. And I think she said they were checking him into the hospital."

"Shit. I need to call Blaze and see how he's doing."

She looked down at her watch. "Maybe you should wait until tomorrow. It's kind of late."

"Poor kid."

"Speaking of getting late, I better get going," she told me as she stood up. "Can I get you anything before I go?"

"Nah, I'm good."

"Okay. I'll be back in the morning to check on you. I left my number on a sticky note on your dresser if you need me before then." She smiled. "Try not to die on me before I get back."

"I'll do my best." Just before she walked out of the room, I called out, "Hazel?"

"Yeah?"

"Thanks."

She smiled that smile I'd come to love as she said, "You're welcome, Shaggy," then shuffled quickly out of the room.

"*Hazel!*" I warned just before my front door slammed shut. I wasn't exactly sure when, but soon, Hazel was going to find out that payback was a bitch.

Over the next couple of days, Hazel continued to do what she could to nurse me back to health, coming several times a day to bring me something to eat and to make sure I'd taken my medicine. With the meds, it didn't take me long to get back on my feet, but I wasn't exactly happy that I was getting better. I'd come to enjoy my time with Hazel and wasn't looking forward to the day she stopped coming by to see me. I'd just have to make the best of the time I had left. When I heard her tap on my front door, I sat up on the bed and turned down the TV.

"Come on in," I shouted.

Seconds later, Hazel walked into the room carrying a paper sack and a Styrofoam cup. I thought she'd be impressed that I'd showered, but she didn't even seem to be fazed by the fact that I no longer looked like death warmed over. From the dark circles under her eyes, I could see that she'd had a long day and she was exhausted. She tried to hide her fatigue, giving me a smile that didn't reach her eyes as she asked, "How ya feeling?"

"I'm hanging in," I answered. "How about you? Long day?"

"Yes … a very long day." She placed the drink and brown paper bag on the bedside table, then plopped down at the foot of the bed. "I'm beat. How about you? Anything interesting with you?'

"Not much. I did call Blaze about Kevin. He said he was home from the hospital," I told her.

"Good. I know you were worried about him."

"Yeah, I was. He seemed like a pretty cool kid. I told Blaze I'd try to be back to work tomorrow."

Her voice went up several octaves as she began to fuss, "No, it's too soon, Clutch. You'll get worse if you push yourself. They can make it a few more days without you." It meant something to me that she cared, but I didn't have a choice; Cotton and Gus were counting on me to get the job done so I could be on my way.

"The sooner I finish in the garage, the sooner I can get back home," I explained.

A look of disappointment crossed her face as she looked down at her lap and started fiddling with the strap of her apron. Without looking up, she said, "Do what you've gotta do, but I think you should give it another day or so."

"Hazel?"

She glanced over to me and mumbled, "Yeah?"

"They're months behind in that garage, and they need me. That's why I'm here. Their top mechanic's laid out, Sunshine. And Blaze needs to be with his boy. All I can think about is the work load building up. I get that you are worried, but if I stay in this room for much longer, I'm going to lose my damned mind. I've gotta get out of here … even if it's just for a little while."

"Okay." She smiled. "Just don't overdo it."

"I won't," I promised. "I'll go in for a couple of hours, and then I'll be back."

She paused for a minute, taking a quiet breath, then asked, "So, when you finish helping them in the garage, you'll head back home?"

"That's the plan."

"Where is home? I mean, if you don't mind me asking."

"You can ask me anything. I grew up in Missouri,

but for the last nine years or so I've been living in Washington."

She leaned back, propping herself up with her arms behind her. "Wow. How did you end up all the way in Washington?"

"I dropped out of college during my junior year after spending the summer out on the road. I was just supposed to be taking a break, but when I ran into Cotton and spent some time at the club, I knew I'd found what I'd been looking for."

"You really dropped out of college just so you could join a motorcycle club?"

"It was where I was meant to be."

"Simple as that, huh?" She smiled.

"Yep. Simple as that. When you know, you know. How about you?"

"I'm a waitress, Clutch. Not much to tell."

"I'm not talking about what you do, Hazel. I want to know what makes you tick. What makes your palms get sweaty and your heart race? What's the one thing you want more than anything in the world? What do you long for late at night when you're lying in bed all alone?"

"You really are a dramatic one." She laughed. "I used to love to dance. I was really pretty good at it, too. I started with ballet when I was just a little girl… maybe four or five, then as I got older, I moved over to contemporary ballet. I loved it, feeling the rhythm of the music, telling a story as I danced, hearing the applause

… but in the end, it just wasn't in the cards for me to dance."

"Why's that?"

"I tried to get into Juilliard, but didn't get asked back for the third audition. I just wasn't good enough."

"So what? What the hell do they know?"

"They know, Clutch. At first I was disappointed, but in the long run, it was the best thing that could've happened."

"Bullshit. If you loved it, you should've kept at it," I told her as I reached for the brown paper sack. I peeked inside and said, "Smells good."

"Louise sent it. It was tonight's special: a grilled chicken sandwich and some fries."

Even though it was getting late, she continued to sit with me while I finished my sandwich. After I was done, we spent another hour talking about my draw to the club and her love of ballet—two completely different worlds, but with us, they seemed to fit. There were differences between me and Hazel, anyone could see them, but the fact was that neither of us seemed to care. We liked being together, and she was finally starting to open up to me. I was getting closer. Each time I was with her, I got another piece of the puzzle. It wouldn't be long before I could piece it all together.

Chapter 11
Olivia

From the moment I'd laid eyes on him, I knew I was in trouble. I'd done my best to resist it from the very start, but nonetheless he'd gotten to me. I'd let my guard down when he was sick, and when I wasn't paying attention, he'd started working his way into my heart. It started with our nightly chats. I'd stop by to see if he was feeling better, and we'd end up visiting for hours, laughing and talking about our day. Those little talks continued long after he'd recovered from the flu. I'd try to resist the temptation of going next door, but when I didn't come over on my own, he'd just end up banging on the wall with some silly excuse to talk. Eventually our nightly rendezvous spilled over into daytime visits, and he'd even started to include Charlie and Hadley. It had become our little routine and I'd come to like it. A lot.

I'd just gotten home from work and barely had time to change into one of my favorite t-shirts and a pair of shorts when Clutch knocked on the door. He'd told me earlier that he was bringing dinner. When I opened the door, I was surprised to see that his hands were full of grocery bags. I took one of the sacks from his hands. "What's all this?"

"I told you I was bringing dinner."

"I thought you meant takeout."

He followed me into the kitchen and placed the remaining bags on the counter as he smiled and said, "No fun in that. I figured we'd make some homemade pizzas. Let Cindy have her way with the toppings."

"You're a brave man. There's no telling what she'll put on it."

He laughed and said, "I figured that, so I limited her options a bit."

We had just started taking everything out of the bags when Charlie walked in and asked, "Do you know where my blue binder is?"

I looked around the kitchen and answered, "No. I haven't seen it."

"I'll find it. I'm sure you-know-who did something with it." He peeked over at the groceries and asked, "We making pizzas for dinner?"

"Yeah. You want to help?" I asked

"Maybe later. I've got to finish up some math homework first," he told me as he walked towards the hall. Seconds later, I heard him fussing at Hadley about taking his binder, immediately followed by the sound of him slamming his bedroom door.

"Do they ever grow out of that?"

Clutch winked and said, "Sorry, darlin'. You're

stuck with it for another ten or twenty years."

"I'll never make it," I giggled. I loved those little winks of his. They got to me every time.

"I don't know about that. They're good kids. You must be doing something right."

"I can't take the credit for that. They've always been great kids."

Once we had everything laid out, Hadley came into the kitchen to help us put on the pizza toppings. Her eyes grew wide when she saw all the different choices and said, "What do I put on it?"

"That's up to you," Clutch answered. "Just remember, you gotta eat it."

"You didn't get any anchovies, did you? I hate those things."

He shook his head. "No anchovies. I'm not much of a fan either."

I leaned over and examined all the choices myself. "Anchovies aren't all that bad."

"Eww," Hadley fussed. Her nose crinkled as she asked, "You actually *like* them?"

"I didn't say that! But there are plenty of people who find them … not gross."

"I think they're gross. And olives, too. No anchovies or olives on the pizzas," Hadley huffed. "We're sticking to the basics tonight."

"I like your way of thinking," Clutch smiled. "Basics are always good."

We spent the next half-hour making up three

different pizzas, and when we put them in the oven to cook, Hadley and Clutch went into the living room to watch TV while I sat with them and folded laundry. I was on my second basket of clothes when Clutch looked over to me and asked, "Are you sure there are only three of you?"

"Yes. Why?"

He glanced down at the laundry basket and said, "Just asking."

"If you are referring to the laundry, Mr. smarty-pants, the kids in this apartment have failed to learn the technique of hanging up a towel or wearing a pair of jeans more than once. So, yeah. I'm stuck doing laundry all the time."

He looked over to Hadley and teased, "Surely she's not talking about you."

Hadley's eyes dropped to her lap. "I always forget, and by the time I remember, the towel is all funky and smells like Char—uh—I mean David's feet."

"It wouldn't smell like feet if you'd hang it up as soon as you were done with it," I fussed. "But you'll figure it out as soon as you have to start doing all the laundry."

"I'm in charge of the vacuuming and dusting," Hadley groaned.

"I think it's time for us to swap," I taunted.

Clutch cut his eyes over to me and smirked as he said, "Don't worry, Cindy. If she starts making you wash clothes, you can borrow my washer and dryer."

"Wait! How come I've never gotten that offer?" I screeched.

Before he could come up with some smart-assed response, the timer went off for the pizzas. He jumped up off the sofa and said, "Saved by the bell."

Charlie finally came out of his room and joined us for dinner. As soon as he saw the pizzas, he said, "These actually look pretty good."

"You doubted our cooking skills?" Clutch asked.

"Yeah … I guess I did. I didn't expect them to actually look like real pizzas," Charlie admitted with a smile.

"Did you finish your math homework?" I asked.

"I finished it. I'm not sure it's right, but I finished it."

"Want me to look over it before we go to bed?" I offered.

"If you want to. It's not that big of a deal. Mrs. O'Neal likes me. If I messed it up, she'll let me fix it," he told me as he took a big bite of pizza.

I looked over at Clutch and smiled, thinking how easily we all fit. The kids were crazy about him, and seeing how good he was with them only made me fall for him even more. He was quickly becoming part of our lives and it terrified me. It wasn't just that I knew so little about him; it was the fact that I'd been lying to him. He knew nothing about our past and the danger that lurked around the corner, and as much as I hated to admit it, deep down I knew it wasn't fair to get him involved.

There was only one thing I could do: I had to end this thing with him before it was too late.

After we finished dinner, the kids went back to their rooms to get ready for bed while I put the laundry away. When I walked back into the kitchen, Clutch was standing at the sink washing the dishes. My heart sank as I stood there staring at him. I liked having him here, sharing the day with him, and I hated the thought of not having him around. I was going to miss him. The way he made me feel safe just by being close, and how easy it was to be with him not only when we were laughing and playing around with the kids, but also the quiet times when we were alone. Mostly I'd miss how alive I felt when he looked at me like I was the only person in the room. It was going to be hard to let go of all of that, but I had no choice. I couldn't take the risk.

When he noticed me standing there, he asked, "You just gonna stand there staring at my ass or are you going to help me put these away?"

"We need to talk."

Without turning around, he replied, "I don't know about that. Sometimes, talking can be overrated. And from the sound of your voice, I figure the talk you want to have is very overrated."

"Clutch," I huffed. "I'm being serious."

"I know. That's the problem," he laughed as he turned to face me. "I've just had a big meal. Not sure I can stomach some heavy conversation right now."

Damn. Why did he have to be so damn good-looking? That sexy little smirk, and those gorgeous green eyes pulled at me, making me want to just forget everything I was about to say. Pulling all the strength I could muster, I finally managed to say, "You're not making this any easier."

"Then I'm doing something right," he teased.

"Look … I'm just going to say it. There's no sense in sugarcoating it. We can't see each other anymore."

His eyebrows furrowed as he studied me for a moment, then he shook his head and said, "I don't know why you say that. I can see you perfectly fine. And I'm liking the shorts. You should wear those more often."

"Really? You're bringing up my shorts right now?"

"You sound surprised. Have you not seen yourself in those shorts? I mean they are sexy as hell, Hazel. You can't really blame me."

I crossed my arms and said, "Let me try this again. Whatever this thing is between us … it's gotta stop. It's just too much. With everything I have going on, I just can't get involved with someone right now."

He took a step closer to me as he said, "Why don't we start there? Why don't you tell me exactly what you have going on, *Hazel*? *All of it*."

And there it was. He was calling me out, and I had no idea how to respond. I stood there frozen as I watched him take another step towards me. His eyes were locked on mine with an intensity I hadn't expected. He wasn't going to let it go, so I did the only thing I knew to do: I lied. "I'm working full time and trying to get my brother and sister through school. I need to be focused on them. I don't have time to be carrying on with some hot guy from next door."

He was just inches from me and I could feel the heat of his breath. "And?"

"And what?"

"All of it." He placed his hand under my chin, gently lifting my face towards his. His green eyes were filled with determination as he said, "I'm not going anywhere, Hazel. Since the minute I first saw you, there hasn't been a day that has gone by that you haven't been on my mind. This thing that you and I have ... I don't know where it's going, but I plan to find out. I'm not letting go, so you might as well go on and tell me what the hell is going on with you and those kids."

"I'm scared," I whispered.

"You're letting your fear keep you trapped in the past. Let me take on some of that fear so we can start moving towards the future."

The intensity of his stare became too much to bear, so I turned away from him as I said, "I don't even know where to start."

Refusing to let me move, he reached for me, pulling me closer to him as he said, "Just start with your name. What's your *real* name?"

Chapter 12
Clutch

It was clear to see that she was nervous. The tension practically rolled off of her as she stood there staring at me with clenched fists, making us both a little on edge. Doing what I could to comfort her, I wrapped my arms around her and pulled her closer to me as I said, "You can trust me. Deep down, you know that."

"I do know that." She rested her head on my chest and whispered, "My name is Olivia Turner. My brother's name is Charlie and my sister's name is Hadley."

I continued to hold her as I said, "See, that wasn't so bad. We're getting there. Now tell me where you're from."

"Boston. We left there a … couple of months ago," she stammered. Her body trembled in my arms. I didn't push; I just waited patiently for her to continue. Finally, she said, "My parents were murdered. The police still aren't sure who did it or why."

When she started to cry, I hugged her tightly and whispered, "I'm sorry, baby. I'm really, really sorry you and those kids had to go through that."

She wiped the tears from her cheek as she looked up at me and said, "There's more. I think the people who killed my parents were trying to get to Charlie and Hadley. They were both in the house when my parents were killed. Charlie saw the men with guns walking down the hall and he freaked out. Before the men could get to them, he snuck Hadley out of the house."

"Smart boy."

"Yes, he was. If he hadn't gotten them out of there …" She started to cry again. "I would've lost them … I would've lost them all."

"But you didn't. They're right here with you. They survived. You all did." I gave her a minute, and then I pushed a little further and said, "I need the rest of it, Olivia."

"It was a few days after the funeral when we started to see a blue van. Someone was following us everywhere. Then, they broke into my apartment. I had no idea what they were looking for, but it scared me and the kids to death. The final straw was the day some strange man showed up at Hadley's school. I think he was there to get her, but she ran to the office before he could get to her."

"That's when you decided to leave?"

"Yes. I packed us up and we just started driving. Ended up here a few months ago."

"And you did this all by yourself?"

"Not exactly. There's a detective back home. He

helped me get the kids enrolled in school, and he's been trying really hard to find the guys who killed my parents."

"What's this detective's name?"

"Detective Brakeman. Why?"

Hating that I knew nothing about this guy, I asked, "Are you sure you can trust him?"

"I can't see why not. He's done everything he could to help us."

I nodded and asked, "Is that all of it?"

She cut her eyes over to me and said, "I don't know. Let's see ... just over three months ago, my parents were murdered. I don't know who killed them or why. But whoever killed them decided to come after my brother and sister, so I packed them up and headed here. During all that, I changed our names, started working at the diner, and found this wonderful apartment. Oh ... and there's the fact that I'm scared to death. Since the day we left Boston, there hasn't been a moment that's gone by that I haven't worried about something happening to those kids. So, yeah ... I'd say that about sums it up." She motioned for the door and said, "So, here's your chance. Run while you can."

I placed my hands on her hips, carefully lifting her up onto the kitchen counter, then stepped between her legs as I said, "I already told you, *Olivia* ... I'm not going anywhere."

"Clutch," she whispered. "It's all just too much. You'd have to be crazy to stick around."

"No. The way I see it, I'd have to be crazy to let you go," I told her as I brought my hands up to the sides of her face. With the flat of my thumb, I gently caressed her cheek, feeling her breath quicken as I leaned closer. "You have no idea how amazing you are."

My thumb trailed across her lower lip. I could feel the heat of her breath against my finger when she softly exhaled. Unable to resist the temptation any longer, I gently pressed my mouth against hers, feeling my world rock beneath me. I wasn't prepared for the simple touch of her lips to set me on fire, an intense heat surging throughout my body. Her soft, delectable lips called out to me, begging to be devoured. Our tongues met, and I became instantly addicted to her intoxicating taste— sweet warmth with a hint of mint. Feeling the same hunger, a light moan vibrated through her chest as her arms wrapped around my neck and her hands quickly began tangling in my hair as she pressed her breasts against my chest. My hands roamed down her back and over the curves of her ass as I thought about how unbelievably perfect she felt in my arms. Remembering we weren't alone, I pulled back, but when I looked down at her lust-filled eyes, I couldn't stop myself from leaning in for another. She opened her mouth with a low moan and I delved deeper, savoring the soft caress of her lips and the quickening of her breath. I was lost, unable to control the storm of desire that was brewing deep inside of me. I wanted her to know there was a promise hidden beneath that kiss—a promise that I intended to keep.

And so it began.

When I heard Charlie's shower cut off, I took a step back, releasing Olivia from our embrace. "No way I'm going anywhere. *Damn,* woman."

Her cheek flushed as she smiled. "You're crazy. You know that, right?"

I winked and said, "You kiss me like that again, and you'll see just how crazy I can be." Seeing that sexy little smile only made me want to kiss her all over again, but knowing the kids were just in the next room, I fought the temptation. The longer I stood there looking at her, the harder it was to resist, so I decided I needed a distraction and said, "Now, are you going to help me do these dishes or what?"

She shook her head and laughed. "You expect me to do dishes after that? No, sir. I'm going to need a cold shower first."

"Baby, I was just getting started. Save the cold shower for later. You're gonna need it," I teased as I walked back over to the sink.

"You're sounding pretty confident over there," she sassed.

"Only because I can back it up. Now get that sexy little ass of yours down from there and help me finish this up."

"Bossy little thing, aren't ya," she teased. She hopped down off the counter and walked over to me. With a satisfied smile, she started drying the dishes I'd already washed and put them away.

It didn't take us long to finish washing them all, and once we were done, I started for the door. Olivia placed her hands on my shoulders as she lifted up on her toes and kissed me on the cheek. She smiled and said, "Thank you for dinner."

"I enjoyed it. The next one is on you. Now, get some sleep," I told her, then kissed her softly on the lips. It was a brief but effective kiss. When I looked up at her, I saw the same longing in her eyes that I'd seen earlier. "Good night, Liv."

"Good night, Clutch," she replied as she watched me walk out the door.

I stood, staring at the closed door, and thought about everything Olivia had told me. It was almost inconccivable that something that fucked up could've happened to them. Not only had they managed to survive, but they'd left everything they knew behind and still ended up on their feet. I had no doubt that was because of Olivia's strength and determination. All on her own, she'd protected those kids from god-knows-who and still managed to find a decent job and put a roof over their heads. Unbelievable.

As soon as I got into my apartment, I grabbed my burner and called Big Mike. Over the years, he'd become a real asset to the club. He had a way with computers and could hack into just about any account. I wanted him to look into Olivia's case and see if he could find some leads. Not only did I want to know who killed their parents, I wanted to know who was after those kids. They meant something to me, and I'd be damned if I was going to let anything happen to them.

As soon as he answered the phone, Big Mike said, "You got Mike."

"Hey there, brother. How's it going over there without me?"

"Clutch? Damn, man. It's been a while. How you doing?" Over the past couple of weeks, I'd been too busy to think about everyone back home, but hearing his voice made everything come rushing back.

"Doing good. Been keeping busy. I've been working my ass off in Gus's garage, but it's paying off. I'll have them caught back up soon."

"Good. It's about time for you to get your ass back home," he scoffed.

"Yeah, can't disagree with you there. I'm ready to get back," I told him. It wasn't exactly a lie, but I wasn't being completely truthful either. "I know it's late, but I've got a favor. Need you to look into something for me."

"Alright. Whatcha got?"

"Need you to work your magic. I need to know everything you can find on Olivia Turner. She's around twenty-six or twenty-seven. She's from Boston, Massachusetts. Her parents were killed just over three months ago. I need to know everything you can find out about the parents: who they worked with, who they'd recently pissed off … whatever you can find on them.

Check the police files. I want to know what they've been able to uncover and see if they have any suspects. Give me everything they've got on file."

"No problem. That all?"

"There is a detective there by the name of Brakeman. He's in charge of the case. See what you can find on him," I added.

"On it," he assured me. "Stay by your phone. If I come across anything, I'll let you know."

"Thanks, man. I'll be waiting."

I hung up and tossed the phone on the coffee table as I dropped down onto the sofa. I was too wound up to sleep just yet, so I grabbed the remote and started flipping through all the different sports channels. I was hoping the hum of the TV would take my mind off of everything, but it didn't help. Every time I closed my eyes, I saw the look on Olivia's face when she told me about her parents. I had no idea who had hurt them, but I wasn't going to stop until I found out.

Chapter 13
Olivia

It was just a single conversation, but I felt like a huge weight had been lifted from my shoulders after I talked to Clutch.

I'd been holding it in for so long, and it felt so good to finally tell him about everything that happened. Over the past few weeks, I'd started to grow feelings for him, and I was afraid he'd be mad at me and I'd lose him once I told him that I'd been lying. But he didn't get mad. He acted like he'd known all along that I was keeping something from him. I shouldn't have been surprised. He was a smart guy. I'm sure he'd heard when the kids slipped up and called out my real name, so it wouldn't take much for him to put two and two together. He stood there and listened to every word as I explained what had happened to my parents and everything I'd gone through to keep the kids safe. He was attentive and understanding and made me feel like I'd done the right thing. When I was done talking, he didn't run for the hills. He didn't even budge from his spot.

Instead, he kissed me.

That kiss—*holy cow!* That surprised me most of all. Seeing the swirl of emotion in his eyes as he stood there staring at me stole my breath. He leaned over me, covering my mouth with a hungry kiss, and everything around me seemed to slip away. The caress of his lips was magic, making me feel like I was walking on air. The worries of my past simply disappeared and gave me a brief reprieve, allowing me for just a moment to consider the possibilities of the future. I'd never felt anything like it, and deep down, I knew it had everything to do with Clutch, and that terrified me.

Over the next few days, Clutch and I explored our newfound relationship, becoming more and more creative with our stolen moments. When the kids weren't around, there were many secret kisses, each one becoming more passionate and demanding than the last. I saw the hunger in his eyes when he looked at me, and it was only a matter of time before he'd want to take that next step. And even though I wanted the same thing, I was terrified. In the past, I hadn't had much experience with men. I had a couple of boyfriends in high school, but I'd only been intimate with one of them. I'd been seeing Timmy for almost three months when we decided to sleep together. Neither of us had been with anyone else, so it was awkward to say the least. After several attempts, it never got any better, so the relationship quickly died out. Then there was Will, my college boyfriend of two years. He came from a wonderful family and studied medicine, and at the time, he was the man I thought I was going to spend the rest of my life with. I was wrong … very wrong. We'd just started our senior year when I found him in bed with my roommate. I was heartbroken, and when I confronted him, he just turned everything around on me, saying I was the reason that he strayed. He never actually said the words, but I always knew it had something to do with our sex life. When we were together, I often felt cold and empty, but I assumed it was just me.

I thought my lack of experience was the reason I never really got anything out of sex, much less orgasmed, but hoped that one day it would get better. Unfortunately, that never happened. Well, it happened for him when he hooked up with my roommate JoAnn. From the way he talked, there were fireworks when they got together—explosive, miraculous fireworks brought down from the heavens above. It had never been like that with me, not even close, and since I'd never felt like that before, I thought there must be something wrong with me. And I continued to think something was wrong with me.

Until the moment Clutch kissed me. For the first time, I understood what Will was talking about when he described those fireworks he'd felt with JoAnn. I'd finally felt them myself when Clutch kissed me, and it kind of freaked me out. It nearly knocked all the wind out of my lungs when he pressed his mouth against mine, and since then, I hadn't been able to think of anything else. I wanted more of those fireworks to the point of completely losing it, but at the same time, I was feeling a little insecure. I wasn't sure that I'd be able to give Clutch those same explosive feelings, so I found myself making excuses not to go to his apartment alone or I'd pull myself away from his kiss before it got too heated. I felt so torn. I wanted him. God, I wanted him more than I'd ever wanted anything else. But at the same time, I was scared I'd lose him. I felt like I was losing my mind.

My sexual frustration was causing me to be on edge, to the point that I was snapping at the kids and even some of my customers. It was getting out of hand, and I had no doubt that Clutch knew he was having an effect on me. I'd seen the little smirk he'd get after we'd kissed. He knew he was getting to me, and he didn't even try to hide it.

I was at my limit, so I decided to take matters into my own hands.

I got off work a few minutes early, so I decided it was time to do a little shopping. I'd been by the store several times, noticing the blacked out windows and neon lights, but until that moment, I'd never dreamed of going inside. When I first walked through the door, I was beyond embarrassed. It was like everyone was watching me as I walked down one of the aisles. I started to lose my nerve, so I turned around and started for the door. I stopped myself when I spotted what I was looking for. Like a teenager buying a bag of pot, I quickly grabbed it and rushed up to the counter. As soon as I paid, I shoved the little white bag down in my purse and headed back to the apartment.

By the time I'd gotten home, the kids had already had their supper and had finished all their homework. Knowing that I'd been a bit moody over the past day or so, they'd locked themselves away in their rooms and were quietly watching TV. I was just about to go apologize for acting like a jerk, when there was a knock at my door. Knowing it was probably Clutch, I shouted, "It's open."

I turned back and watched as he stepped into the apartment looking as irresistible as ever with his sexy little smile and those jeans that made it damn near impossible for me not to stare at his ass. His long-sleeved t-shirt fit snug under his cut, making me want to run my fingers over the muscles of his chest. I'd decided he'd worn it just to torment me and that only fueled my irritated mood.

With his eyes trained on mine, he started in my direction and when he reached me, his arms wrapped around my waist, pulling me closer as he began nuzzling my neck with light kisses. Goosebumps prickled my skin as he worked his way up to my ear and whispered, "Hey there, Sunshine."

"Hey," I replied as my body melted into a pile of mush in his arms.

He continued to trail kisses along my jaw until he reached my lips, then softly pressed his mouth against mine. The scent of his cologne. The feel of his body. It was all too much. My senses were being seduced yet again and I couldn't think straight. When he deepened the kiss, sending my need for him to an entirely new level of insanity, I placed the palms of my hands on his chest and gave him a quick shove.

He looked down at me, noticing the disgruntled frown on my face, and grinned as he asked, "What's with the look?"

Oh, he knew damn well why he was getting the look, and he thought it was funny. I, on the other hand, did not. I pointed to my face and growled, "This look? Is this the look you are referring to?"

"Yeah, that'd be the one."

I stood there glaring at him. I had a million thoughts running through my head, but I couldn't make sense of any of them. How could I tell him that he was turning me into some sex-starved lunatic? There was no way to tell him without sounding completely demented, so I just said, "Nothing. I had a bad day."

"Bullshit. Tell me."

"There's nothing to tell," I answered as I tried to turn away from him. "I'm just tired, that's all."

He reached for me, stopping mid-step, and said, "I'll get it out of you one way or another, Liv. Make it easy on yourself and just tell me what's going on in that head of yours."

"Nothing. I don't want to talk about it," I snapped. He pulled me over to him and began nibbling along the curve of my neck again, and that was all it took. The dam broke and there was little I could do to stop it. "Okay! That's it! You want to know, then I'll tell you. I'm sexually frustrated, Clutch. Every time you touch me, I feel like a horny teenager on crack, and I'm going to completely lose it if we don't do something about it soon. Clutch, I need to get laid ... like, *bad* ... but at the same time, the thought of being with you scares me to death."

"You want to tell me why that scares you?"

I fanned my hand in his direction and said, "Because you're all that. All muscled up and sexy as hell. I'm sure you've been with all kinds of women and done all kinds of stuff, while I'm sitting here with—"

He placed his hand on the nape of my neck, which silenced me, and said, "Don't give my past a second thought, Liv. Since the minute I laid my eyes on you, I haven't given a second thought to anyone else."

"It's just ..." I stopped when I couldn't find the right words.

His eyes locked on mine. "You just don't get it. You're amazing, Olivia. It blows me away that you don't get that. The way your body lights up whenever I just get close to you ... I have no doubt when that time comes, it will be worth the wait."

"I guess I'm not doing as well as you are with the waiting." I pointed to my purse, and before I had time to think about what I was saying, I said, "I even went to some crazy store and bought ..." I stopped myself. I wanted to go back in time and erase those words from my lips, but it was too late. He was already eyeballing my purse and making a beeline for it. I rushed over to stop him as I shouted, "Stop! It's nothing."

He'd already started peering inside, and when he saw the little white bag, he snatched it out of my purse and with a big goofy grin on his face, he asked, "What'd you get, Olivia?"

"Nothing. Give it to me!" I screeched as I tried to take the bag from his hand.

He lifted it over his head and laughed as he said, "Oh, this has to be good. I don't think I've ever seen you so worked up."

"Just give it to me, Clutch. I shouldn't have bought the stupid thing anyway. It was a bad idea, and..."

He shook his head and brought the bag down just enough for him to take a look inside. There was no doubt that he enjoyed tormenting me. That big goofy smile on his face gave him away and it only got bigger when he started to look inside the bag. His eyes lit up when he finally saw what I'd bought and he snickered. "Well, lookie here. It's hot pink."

"Clutch, just give it to me."

"I bet you can have all kinds of fun with this little sucker," he tormented.

"Clutch!" I shouted again.

"Oh, baby. Don't be embarrassed about it. I'm glad you got it. You've been driving everyone nuts with your little moods. I'd like to be the one that took the edge off, but I can wait until you're ready for that. For now, maybe this will do the trick," he said with a chuckle.

"My little moods?" I snapped.

"Yeah, your little moods. You've been wound up tighter than a girdle on a Baptist minister's wife on Sunday."

"You are an ass! Now give me the stupid bag."

"You're cute when you get flustered." His eyes danced with mischief as he handed the sack over to me and said, "I've gotta say. I like that I'm getting to you. I bet this will help."

"Just stop."

"What? You know that in the nineteenth century, doctors used them to treat hysteria in women."

"Hysteria? Really?" I huffed. "So, now I'm hysterical?"

"Well…" he smirked.

I dropped my head into my hands and groaned, "Just please stop talking. It's bad enough you found my vibrator. Hearing you talk about it is making my skin hurt."

"Oh, come on. Don't make a big deal of it. Just have fun with it."

Hadley popped her head into the room and asked, "Have fun with what?"

As soon as I heard her voice, I closed the little white bag and shoved it in the drawer next to me. I stood in front of it with my arm crossed and smiled as I said, "Clutch was thinking of taking us all bowling."

"Bowling? I haven't been bowling in forever. That would be fun. When are we going?" she asked.

"I don't know. We were just throwing out some ideas," Clutch jumped in, "but, we'll let you know."

"Okay." She looked back over to me. "Can I borrow your nail polish remover?"

"Yeah, sweetie. It's under the bathroom sink. Just put it back when you're done," I told her.

As soon as she left the room, Clutch whispered, "Nice save." Then he started laughing, and once he started, he couldn't stop—which made me start to laugh, and before it was all said and done, we were both laughing hysterically.

With tears streaming down my face, I stammered, "You are so bad."

"You have no idea. You have fun playing with your little toy. Just remember … someday soon, I get my turn."

By the time Clutch had gone home and the kids were in bed, I was exhausted. I got comfortable on the sofa and turned the TV down low, hoping that I'd be able to finally get some sleep. I hadn't been lying there long when I found myself staring at the drawer in the kitchen where my little purchase was tucked away. I rolled my eyes and turned back to face the television as I thought about how asinine it was for me to buy something like that. Since I'd never owned one, I was a little curious about how the stupid thing even worked. It was silly. There was no way I was ever going to use that crazy thing. Was I? I rolled over on my side and tried to block it from my thoughts, but only a few moments later, I found myself staring at that same damn drawer. Like they say: curiosity killed the cat.

Chapter 14
Clutch

It was still pitch black outside when I got up for work, well before Olivia and the kids were up and rolling, so I did my best to be quiet on my way out, so I wouldn't wake them. When I got to the bottom of the stairs, Cyrus was there opening the diner. He saw that I was about to leave and motioned me over to him.

"Cup of coffee before you head out?" he offered.

"Yeah, I could use a cup or two," I answered as I followed him inside. I waited for him to turn on all the lights before I went to sit behind the counter.

After a few minutes of stirring around in the kitchen, he came out front and started up the coffeemaker. When it was all set, he asked, "How's it going down at the garage?"

"We're making some progress. Hope to have things wrapped up in a few weeks."

"Good to hear. I'll be sure to let Gus know," he told me as he poured us both a cup of coffee and placed it on the counter. "And how are things going with Hazel?"

And there it was: the real reason he'd wanted to

talk. I knew he'd been looking out for her and there was no doubt that he'd seen us talking and wondered what the hell was going on with us.

"I'd say things are going good with Hazel. Very good, in fact."

"You know … she's a good one. She's a hard worker and she's great with those kids."

"I'm well aware of that. More than you know."

"So she means something to you?"

"Absolutely," I assured him as I took a drink of my coffee.

"I was hoping you'd say that. She's been different since you've been around. She's happy. I'd like to see her stay that way."

"You and me both. I don't know anyone who deserves it more than she does. I plan to do whatever it takes to keep a smile on her face."

"I had a good feeling about you. Turns out I was right. I like it when I'm right," he chuckled. "I've been doing what I can to keep an eye on her and those kids. The club has them covered. I know something's up with her, but haven't been able to find out anything. She tell you?"

"I appreciate that, brother. She told me that someone killed her parents a few months ago. She's worried whoever did it decided to come after the kids," I explained.

"What do you think?"

"Hard to tell just yet. I've got my guy looking into

it, but either way, I'm not taking any chances."

"Let me know what you find out. And if you need anything, just say the word."

"Thanks, Cyrus. I better get moving. You'll be getting busy soon."

"Don't I know it. But busy means money, so I can't complain. Have a good one, brother."

"Will do," I told him as I drank the last of my coffee and headed towards the back door. It was a relief to know the club had her back, and I was glad we were on the same page with keeping her and the kids safe. When I stepped outside, something caught my eye by the dumpsters. It looked like a person curled up on their side, and when I stepped closer, I quickly realized that it was Olivia's friend, the homeless guy she's been keeping tabs on. I knelt down beside him and discovered that he was covered in blood and bruises.

I reached out and touched him on the shoulder. "Hey ... you okay?"

"Just need to ... sit here a ... minute," he stammered. He didn't open his eyes. I'm not even sure that he could with all the swelling. Also, his voice was strained, making it clear that he was in a lot of pain. His left eye was completely swollen shut and his knuckles were bleeding on both hands. From the look of his wounds, they must've wailed on him with a tire iron, but he'd done his best to put up a fight.

"You're pretty banged up, man. I need to get you to a hospital."

He winced as he shook his head and moaned, "No … no hospital."

When I noticed the blood oozing from his gut, I told him, "You need to get checked out. You're bleeding."

"Already know that. No hospital," he growled.

"Okay, then I'm going inside to get some help," I told him as I stood up. I rushed inside and called out, "Cyrus! Need you, brother."

"Coming!" he shouted. Seconds later he came barreling out of the kitchen and followed me outside. "What is it?"

"That guy Hazel has been helping out, he's been beat up pretty bad. Probably needs to see a doctor or something, but he isn't budging."

"Sam can be a stubborn old fool," Cyrus grumbled. When he got over to the dumpster, he looked down at the broken man in front of him and mumbled several curses under his breath. Finally, he bent down and said, "Sam, you alright?"

His breathing was strained as he said, "Been better. Sorry for causing … you trouble."

Cyrus lifted Sam's shirt and gasped when he saw the knife wound that covered his chest. "Fuck, Sam. Who did this to you?"

"Group of damn kids … hit me from behind," he muttered.

Getting frustrated, Cyrus snapped, "Don't even try that bullshit, Sam. I've seen what you can do. You and I both know there's no way a group of damn kids could have taken you, unless you let them. You're lucky they didn't kill you. Hell, they may have already gotten you halfway into the grave."

"Gonna be ... fine," he moaned.

Sam was looking worse by the minute. He was struggling to talk and his breathing was getting shallow. Worried that we might lose him, I warned, "We've gotta get him to the doctor, Cyrus. He's gonna bleed out if we don't."

"Let me tell Louise what's going on and get the keys to the truck. He won't go to the damn hospital, so we'll carry him over to the clubhouse and let Mack have a look at him. He can stitch him up and get him back on his feet," Cyrus explained. He looked over to Sam and said, "Not that you have a choice, but are you gonna be alright with that?"

"Yeah," he agreed.

Once Cyrus returned with the keys to his truck, it took both of us to load Sam in the back seat of his extended cab pickup. For his size, he weighed more than either of us thought, but we managed to get him into the truck without causing him too much pain. Before we pulled out of the lot, Cyrus turned to me and asked, "You planning to give Hazel a heads-up about this? You know she's got a soft spot for him."

Sam groaned from the back of the truck and said, "No. Don't. She will ... worry."

"Yeah. He's right. Don't want to worry her just yet.

Let's get him fixed up and then we'll go from there."

He nodded, then drove on to the clubhouse. Cyrus called ahead to let Mack know we were on the way so he'd have time to prepare. When we pulled through the gate, it was still early, so not many of the brothers were around. By the time he'd parked the truck, there was a man in his early thirties waiting for us at the front door. The guy looked like he'd just crawled out of bed with his wrinkled t-shirt and baggy jeans, but that didn't stop him from rushing over to the truck to help us.

"Need a hand?" he asked.

Cyrus opened the truck door and started reaching for Sam as he said, "I think we got it, Mack."

I helped Cyrus get him out of the back seat and then followed him to the back of the clubhouse to the infirmary. He'd already gotten everything set up, and when we walked in, Mack pointed over to the gurney and said, "Just lay him there."

As I looked around, I noticed the room was similar to ours back home: two gurneys in the back, and L-shaped cabinets along the wall filled with gauze, medicine, and medical tools. It wasn't much different than any other doctor's office except for the lack of medical degree hanging on the wall. Sam looked up at him and said, "You're just a kid."

"Looks can be deceiving." Mack smiled. "I'm going to need to take off your shirt and check your wounds." Sam nodded and did his best to prop himself up long enough for us to get off his jacket and blood-soaked clothes. Once he laid back down, Mack winced when he saw the long, jagged cut that crossed Sam's chest. "Damn, man. They got you good." He leaned in closer and pressed his fingers against the cut as he said, "Fortunately, it's just a deep graze. Doesn't look like they got deep enough to hit any major arteries or organs, but you're gonna need stitches. A lot of them."

"What do you need us to do?" I asked.

"We need to get him cleaned up before I work on him," Mack explained. "There's betadine and gauze in the cabinet behind you."

For someone who'd been living on the streets, he was much cleaner than I'd anticipated. Even though he was in a bad spot, he'd obviously tried his best to take care of himself. Once I found the betadine and gauze, I handed them over to Mack. It took him a while to disinfect the wound, but then he was ready to get to work. He looked down at Sam and, with concern in his voice, said, "Sam, I'm going to give you something for the pain. Couple of shots to numb you before I start stitching you up." Sam nodded and then Mack looked over at us. "It's going to be a while. Breakfast should be about ready if you want to go grab something to eat."

"Breakfast sounds good, but hurry this shit up, brother. I gotta get back to work before Louise blows a fucking gasket."

"On it," Mack answered as he started giving Sam his first shot.

I followed Cyrus down the hall. When we walked

into the kitchen, three of their girls were busy making a huge breakfast. They were young, early twenties—if that, and even though it was only six-thirty in the morning, they were already dressed to the nines. Just like our girls back home, they never missed an opportunity to catch the wandering eye of one of the brothers. Unfortunately, at that moment, none of the brothers even seemed to notice; they were sitting down at the table talking back and forth to one another as they waited to be served their breakfast. The last thing they seemed to notice were the girls in their ten-inch heels.

When we approached the table, one of the older guys looked up at Cyrus and said, "What are you still doing here? Louise is gonna have your ass, brother."

"Don't you know it, but she'll just have to get over it. I had something come up," he groaned. "Shouldn't be too bad. Little Dan is there. I reckon they'll make do for another hour or so." Cyrus motioned his hand over to me and said, "Y'all met Clutch yet?"

"You the kid from the Washington chapter that they got helping out in the garage?" one of the men asked. The grimace on his face reminded me of Cotton, especially with his salt and pepper hair and goatee. They looked a bit similar, but he was wider than Cotton and maybe a little older.

"Yeah. That's me," I replied as I took a seat at the table next to Cyrus.

"That's Murph, our Sergeant of Arms. The handsome, bald fellow to your left is T-Bone, and the

little guy at the end of the table is our enforcer, Runt."
Cyrus chuckled. Runt was at least six-eight and weighed
about three hundred and sixty pounds without an ounce
of fat anywhere on him. Anyone could see that he was a
force to be reckoned with.

I nodded and said, "Good to meet ya."

"You Road Captain?" T-bone asked with his slick
head shining under the bright lights.

"I am."

His eyebrows furrowed as he studied me. "I figured
you'd be older."

"Is that right?"

Just like Gus, the minute he saw me, I could see
that he was trying to figure me out. It was no secret that
I was younger than most Road Captains, but I'd earned
my way—Dub made sure of that—so I didn't feel the
least bit slighted when he questioned me. I chose to just
let it go and watch quietly as the girls placed the food on
the table. Once they were done, I followed the others'
lead and started to make myself a plate of eggs and
bacon. When I was done, I said, "Looks good."

I felt a hand drape around my shoulder as a female
voice purred, "Glad you like it, handsome. Let me know
if you need anything else."

I glanced over to her, seeing the look of lust in her
eyes, and said, "I'll keep that in mind."

Runt leaned forward and asked, "You making any
progress in that damn garage?"

"Yeah. We're getting there. I'd hoped to be a little

further along by now, but we'll get it done. Should have everything on track in a few weeks."

"Blaze has had a time of it since Duggar's been out of commission, but he's only got a few more days 'til he'll be released back to work," Cyrus explained.

We continued to talk about the garage. I had to dodge a few questions about the new pipeline, figuring Gus would give them the information when he was good and ready. Just as we were finishing up our breakfast, Mack came into the kitchen looking for us. He walked over to us and said, "I've got him all stitched up, but he needs to get some rest and something decent to eat. I think he should stay here for a day or so until we get him back on his feet."

"I'll run it by Gus, make sure he's okay with it," Cyrus told him.

"Already did," Mack replied. "He can stay in the back until his vision has cleared and he can get around a little better. Figured I'd get one of the girls to save him a plate of breakfast for when he wakes up."

"Thanks, brother. I appreciate that," I told him. "I'll be back later to check on him. Just let me know if you need anything."

"I got him." Mack smiled. "He's a good man. Hate to see that he's fallen on hard times."

"The real pisser of it is, it doesn't have to be this way for him," Cyrus clipped. "He's living on the streets because he chooses to. I don't understand it. I've tried talking to him, but he's just too damn thick-skulled to listen to anyone."

"Why would he choose to live on the streets?"

"He's not one to talk about it, but he was married to a woman named Clara. He met her when he'd come home from deployment. From what he's said, they had it good. He loved her. Tried to give her everything down to the white picket fence. They had a daughter named Faith. She's a good kid. She was just fifteen when everything went to hell. Sam was deployed when Clara died. When he finally made it back home, he wouldn't step foot in their house or have anything to do with his family. Faith moved in with her grandmother, but she never gave up on him. Tried everything she could to get him some help ... counseling and doctors, but he refused treatment every damn time. Been like that for years."

I looked at Cyrus. "That's rough, man. Wish there was something more we could do."

"You can't help those who aren't willing to help themselves, brother, but we'll do what we can," he grunted back. "Maybe he'll come around and decide he has something worth living for. For now, let's just get him back on his feet."

Cyrus took me back to the diner to get my bike, and while I was there, I decided to check in on Olivia. When I walked in, she was standing at the counter taking an order from an elderly lady and her husband. Her eyes lit up and her lips curved into a sexy smile when she saw me walking towards her. The closer I got, the wider her smile became, making me want to pull her close. When I finally got to her, I leaned in and whispered in her ear, "Hey there, Sunshine."

"Hey." She blushed—and that's when I knew. I took a step back, studying her expression just to be sure, and then I couldn't stop myself from grinning like the Cheshire cat. She immediately cocked her head to the side and asked, "What?"

"You feeling better?" I teased.

"What do you mean?" she asked defensively. When it finally dawned on her that I really did know what she'd been up to, she brought her hand up to her face and tried to cover her embarrassed smile. Just seeing her eyes dance with mischief had my dick raging against the zipper of my jeans.

"From the looks of that smile, you enjoyed it," I chuckled. "Satisfaction looks good on you, babe."

She started walking away and when she got several steps in front of me, she looked back over her shoulder as she snapped, "We *are not* going to talk about this now or ever!"

"Mmm-hmm," I mumbled as I followed her towards the back of the diner. She was walking so fast that her long, brown hair whirled around her when she turned the corner. I reached out for her, pulling her over to me as I laughed. "Where you going, Sunshine?"

Her face turned beet red as she fussed, "Clutch! Seriously. I'm working."

"I'm sure your customers are glad to see their old

Hazel is back ... free of all that pent-up sexual frustration," I heckled.

Then she surprised me.

With a lustful look in her eyes, she turned to face me. She took a step towards me, closing the distance between us, as she placed her hand on my shoulder and lifted up on her toes. She leaned into me, pressing her breasts against my chest as she brought her lips closer to my ear and seductively whispered, "I wouldn't say I was free of *all* my frustration. Not even close." She brushed the hair from my eyes and said, "I've gotta get back to work, Shaggy."

She placed a gentle kiss on my cheek and sauntered back over to her table, intentionally swaying her hips much more provocatively than usual. Fuck. With just one look, she had me spinning. I left the diner in a complete daze, and for the life of me, I couldn't get that look on her face out of my head. Just the thought of her using that fucking vibrator had me coming apart at the seams, and I spent the entire damn day at the garage fighting a fucking hard-on. I couldn't get out of there fast enough.

When we were finally done for the day, I headed straight home, and once I was there, I didn't waste any time getting into the shower. I'd hoped the cold water would take the edge off, but every time I closed my eyes, I pictured Olivia with that heated look in her eyes, reaching for that little pink vibrator. When I thought about her slipping it deep inside her and rubbing it against her G-spot, I couldn't take it any longer. I turned the water to hot and took my throbbing dick in my hand, gripping my fingers tightly around my pulsing shaft. I needed to feel the bite as I started to move my hand up and down my thick cock. As soon as I closed my eyes, I was bombarded with visions of Olivia's smooth, bare skin ... her hand trailing across her perfect, round breast, reaching for her erect nipple, twisting it gently between the tips of her fingers. My breath quickened as I imagined her writhing against the soft cotton sheets with her little whimpers and moans echoing through the room. With each vision, my hand moved faster, gripped tighter and every stroke had me closer to the edge. My dick pulsed in my hand when I imagined the expression on her face as she pressed the small, pink vibrator against her clit, feeling the intensity of her orgasm surging through her body. The erotic blush of skin. Her thighs clenching. Her toes curling. Fuck. That's all it took. My breath caught, and I came long and hard. Moments later, I stepped out of the shower with my dick still standing at full salute, taunting me with the knowledge that, unlike Olivia, my sexual frustration had only just begun.

Chapter 15
Olivia

"That friend of yours was awfully nice to help me out," Sam told me. "Don't reckon I'd still be around if it wasn't for him finding me like he did."

"I'm just glad he was able to help," I told him. "I wanted to come see you, but Clutch told me that you didn't think it was a good idea for me to come."

"Didn't want you to see me like that, doll. I was in pretty rough shape."

His face was covered in dark blue and green bruises, and the cuts and scrapes on his hands and arms were far from healed. I couldn't begin to imagine how bad he looked the morning Clutch found him by that dumpster. When Clutch described everything that had happened, I was heartbroken for Sam. He'd been through so much, and I hated the thought of someone hurting him, especially when it was done in such a vicious way. Sam was unarmed and was no real threat to the guys who attacked him, but they didn't care. They took sport in hurting him, taking turns hitting and kicking him just for fun, which made the whole thing that much worse. I wanted to be there for him, but when I mentioned going to see him at the clubhouse, Clutch told me that he promised Sam that he'd keep me away until he'd gotten better. I wasn't exactly happy about it, but I understood that they both had good intentions. It meant the world to me that Clutch had been there for Sam, but I wasn't surprised; Clutch had a way of always being there when you needed him.

"Well, you still need to get some rest and take care of yourself. Please don't be in a hurry to leave the clubhouse. Stay long enough to get back on your feet," I pleaded. He still couldn't stand up straight, much less walk without a limp, and I was worried that he was pushing himself too soon.

"I'll stick around for a few more days, but I don't want to outstay my welcome," he smiled. "Those boys don't want an old fart like me lying around there."

"I doubt that. I'm sure they don't mind you being there. Where will you go when you leave?"

"The shelter on Second Street. Cyrus got it all worked out for me to stay there for a bit," he answered.

I hated the thought of him being all alone, but I couldn't think of any other options. I knew there wasn't much else I could do. "Just please take care of yourself, Sam. I like having you around," I said. "So, Mr. Stubborn. How about a sandwich or a bowl of soup?"

"Whatever you've got will be fine," he said and smiled.

"Okay. I'll see what I can scrounge up."

I went back to the kitchen window and placed an order for him. When I came back out, I found Clutch sitting at the front counter. He was still wearing his work clothes and there was a smudge of grease on his chin, making him look even sexier. I couldn't figure it out. How did dirt and grime make him look even better? I was losing it. He smiled when he saw me walking over to him and said, "Hey there, Sunshine."

"Hey there, Shaggy," I teased as I took a napkin and cleaned the grease from his jaw. "How was your day?"

"Long, but better now. What about you?"

"I had an interesting offer from Louise earlier today," I started. "I'm not sure where it came from, but I was thinking the kids might enjoy it."

"What kind of offer?" he asked, sounding intrigued.

"She's having a get-together for her grandkids and some of their friends. They are going to do a bonfire and campout at her place. The kids all go to school together, so she thought Hadley and Charlie might like to tag along."

With his eyebrow raised and a sexy smirk spreading quickly across his face, he said, "I'd say that sounds like a very interesting offer."

"I have to talk to the kids first. It sounds like a lot of fun for them, but you never know ... They may not want to go," I told him.

"Won't know until you ask."

"I guess you're right." I placed my elbows on the

counter and leaned into him. "But you know … if they *do* go, that means we have a night to ourselves."

"Can't think of a better way to spend a night. Talk to them. Let me know what they say."

"Talk to who?" Charlie asked as he walked up beside Clutch.

"What are you doing down here?" I asked. "I thought you were watching TV with Hadley."

"She was watching some kid's show. There's only so much I can take of that goofy crap, so I thought I'd come down here and see how things were going with you." He sat down at the counter. He looked back over to me and asked, "So, who do you have to talk to?"

"You, actually. I was talking to Louise earlier. She's having a get-together for Kyleigh and Logan this weekend. They are going to have some friends over for a bonfire and a campout. They'll grill out, do some fishing, and play games. She wanted to know if you and Hadley would like to go."

His eyes lit up with excitement as he said, "That sounds cool. I bet Devin and Jace will be there, too."

"So you want to go?"

"Yeah, it'll be awesome. Logan can be a pain in the ass, but his friends are cool. Can we go?" he asked, sounding hopeful.

I was tickled to see him excited about being with some new friends. "Sure. I think it will be fun."

"Awesome. I'll go tell Hadley about it. She's going to be stoked," he told us as he stood up to leave. Before he left, he leaned over to Clutch and grinned as he said, "Maybe while we're gone, you can take *Hazel* out for a good time, too."

"I'm sure I can come up with something," Clutch declared.

Once he was gone, I said, "That went better than I thought."

"It'll be fun for them and Louise will make sure of it."

"Order up," Little Dan called from the kitchen.

"Duty calls," I told him as I leaned over and planted a big kiss on his lips. "You want me to put in an order for you?"

"Nah. I'm good. I'm just gonna head upstairs for a shower." He stood to leave. "I'll grab something later." He looked over to the back table and smiled as he said, "Tell Sam I said hello."

"I will," I answered as he started towards the back door. Once he was gone, I turned to get Sam's order from the serving window. When I got over to Sam, I noticed that he had a big, contagious smile on his face. I placed his food on the table and asked, "What are you so happy about?"

"Does the old heart good to see you happy," he answered. "It's been a long time since I've seen you smile like that."

He'd said sweet things to me like that before, but this time was different. It wasn't what he'd said that had me worried, but the way he was looking at me. From the distant look in his eyes, I could tell that he wasn't thinking clearly as he spoke. I stepped closer, placing my hand on his shoulder as I replied, "Yeah, I'm pretty happy these days, but I'm a little worried about you. Are you feeling okay, Sam?"

His back straightened as he sat there quietly studying me for a moment, then his face grew pale. His eyes dropped to his lap as he mumbled under his breath. He ran his hands over his face, then finally looked back up at me. "I'm fine. Just a little tired I guess. I … uh … It's just you and that boy seem to be getting along. Happy to see you doing well. You're a sweet girl. You deserve to be happy."

"We're doing alright. Well, today we are. Who knows what the future holds." I smiled.

His eyes grew intense as he said, "Hold on to the good, Hazel. Hold on tight." He looked down at his plate of food and started eating, letting me know that he was done talking for the moment. I left him to eat in peace, but continued to check on him until my shift was over. I couldn't help but worry about him. Over the past few weeks, he'd become very important to me. He was a good man. I could see it in his eyes and in the way that he talked about things that were important to him, but he'd lost his way. I just had to believe that he'd eventually figure things out and get back on his feet. I was glad to know that I wasn't the only one who felt that way about him; Cyrus also had a soft spot for him and was doing what he could to help. He'd made arrangements for Dan to take him back to the clubhouse after he finished his dinner. He'd gotten him a room set up and hoped that being around the guys might actually do him some good. When Sam finished his sandwich, Dan pulled his truck up to the front door to get him. Sam waved goodbye, and once he was gone, I headed upstairs to put the kids to bed.

When I finally got in bed myself, I couldn't sleep. Like the pea in the princess's bed, thoughts of Clutch had me tossing and turning all night, and the next few nights weren't much better. It was agony. Each hour seemed to drag into the next as I waited for my night alone with Clutch. I was a wreck. One minute I was elated by the thought of finally getting to take that next step with him, but then, in a flash, I was slammed with a bottle full of nerves. I did what I could to distract myself with idle jobs around the apartment or taking the kids shopping for things that they'd need for camping, but nothing helped. Clutch was constantly on my mind. It didn't help matters that since I'd told him about the camping trip, he'd been oddly distant. He'd started working later and later each night, cutting our nightly visits into quick dinners or short chats about our day. His lack of attention was absolute torture.

I was really starting to miss those little stolen moments, so I decided it was time to give him a little push—and I wasn't exactly subtle about it either. I paraded around the apartment in his favorite cutoff shorts when he came over for dinner, and the minute I saw him walking into the diner, I would unfasten an extra button on my uniform. I'd smile and flirt, but no change. When that didn't work, I started making excuse after pathetic excuse just to touch him, even if it was just to get a piece of lint off of his t-shirt. Unfortunately for me, he wouldn't take the bait, and I was left feeling like an idiot and … a tad desperate. Something had to change—and fast.

Chapter 16
Clutch

She was killing me ... absolutely, fucking killing me. I couldn't even be in the same room with her without getting a damn hard-on, and she wasn't helping one bit. I had known she was doing it on purpose—the sexy little smiles and the nonchalant flips of her hair, wearing those sexy-as-hell cutoff shorts that showed off her long, lean legs, and that extra hint of cleavage she was sporting whenever I was around. Fuck. I wanted her so bad, my teeth hurt, and I knew if I got too close, I'd lose the last of my restraint. So I did the only thing I could: I kept my distance. I spent extra hours in the garage and took a few long rides through the city, whatever I could to get my mind off that hungry look in her eyes.

I finally got the distraction I needed when Big Mike called.

I'd just finished lunch and gotten back to the garage when my burner started ringing. When I saw that it was him calling, I quickly answered, "What did you find?"

"You got yourself an interesting one here, Clutch.

A college graduate. Good job. Nice apartment. Pretty little thing, too," he started.

"I know all that, Mike. What else you got?" I pushed.

"Her dad was one of the top real estate agents in Boston. A few years back, his company bought up several lots downtown. He was working with the mayor and the city council to renovate the area. Some cool new restaurants, a coffee shop, and a couple of those girly stores that sell t-shirts and shit. From what I can tell, it was going good. Really good. People were buying into it, and the area is booming now. It's doing just what he said it would do, and people are starting to move into some of the older homes and they're fixin' them up."

"All that sounds legit. So how did he end up with a bullet in his head?"

"Still not exactly sure. I do know that a man by the name of Hanson from New York got wind of the new development. He came in with an offer to buy up several of the empty lots, but Turner wasn't interested. He didn't like the fact that he wanted to open a Gentleman's club and a couple of bars. It wasn't what he was going for, so he didn't take the offer, even though Hanson was offering above asking price— almost double—and it would've made Turner's company a killing."

"So the money didn't matter to him?"

"Apparently not. He kept the offer hidden under a mountain of paperwork. His partner wanted him to push it through. His son even went behind Turner and wrote up a contract. They would've made a killing on it."

"So you think the business partner and Hanson had something to do with the murder?"

"Can't say for sure. Perry had a guilty conscience for sure. The suicide note had a message for Olivia. After a bunch of mumbo jumbo crap, he said to tell her that he was sorry."

"Fuck. What about his son?"

"He'd been working with the company for a couple of years. I'd say he's doing alright. Got a BMW and a penthouse apartment," he said and chuckled.

"Sounds like he's doing better than alright."

"No doubt. I'm still digging. I'll see what else I can find on him. Also still looking into this Hanson guy. He's a high roller, and I'm trying to see if I can find any shady connections. He started off small, but he's made a fortune by buying and selling different businesses around the country. There's not much on him."

"Gotta wonder why a high roller would want to set up shop in a suburb of Boston. Why was that spot so important?"

"I don't know, brother, but I'll find out."

"What did you find on Detective Brakeman?"

He let out a sigh. "Brakeman looks clean, man. Not a lot on him. He's got a place out on the eastside of town with his wife and two kids. Seems like a typical all-American family to me, but those are always the ones with skeletons in the closet. I'll see what else I can come up with."

"Thanks, Mike. I appreciate it. How are things going back at home?" I asked.

"It's going. Cotton and Guardrail have been working on the new pipeline, trying to get everything ready to roll. Waiting on Nitro to get the shipment lined up," he explained. "When you planning on heading back?"

"Things are moving along in the garage, so it shouldn't be much longer. But I've got some other things to tend to before I can head back."

"Like this Olivia?" he chuckled.

"None other. Get back to me as soon as you can, Mike. I need to know what the hell is going on."

"I'll have more in a day or so. I'll be in touch," he replied as he hung up the phone.

I put my phone in my back pocket and tried to focus on work. The garage was buzzing. Several new faces were there doing what they could to help out Blaze. During their last doctor's visit, Kevin's bloodwork had been off. The doctors decided to run some more tests, so Blaze had been at the hospital with him most of the day. I'd managed to get the entire engine pulled out of the truck I was working on and had finished most of the disassemble when he finally got to the garage.

He gave me a half smile as he walked over to me and said, "You getting anywhere with that piece of shit?"

"Slowly but surely. This one might do me in," I groaned. He quickly glanced at the progress I'd made and nodded with satisfaction as he leaned against the hood of the car. I looked over to him and asked, "How did it go at the hospital?"

"I don't know, Clutch. They want to run more fucking tests, and I'm sick and fucking tired of seeing my son treated like a goddamn pin cushion. I just want some answers. I just don't see why they can't just tell me something."

"Figure they want to be sure before they tell you anything, brother. It's hard, but when they are done, you'll know for sure."

"That's the hardest part. Not knowing. If I just knew, I could prepare either way. I need to be able to get my head straight," he grumbled.

I placed my hand on his shoulder and said, "I wish I had the answer, but only time is going to give you that. Just try to keep it together a little longer. You'll know more soon."

"Never been good with that whole patience thing," he admitted. "I appreciate you staying late this week."

"Don't mention it," I told him as I looked at the clock. It was almost time for Louise to pick up the kids. "I've gotta head out, but if you need anything, just give me a shout."

"Will do." When I walked out the door, he shouted, "Have a good weekend."

"Planning on it."

The kids were supposed to leave around seven, and since it was already after dark when I got back to the apartment, I knew I didn't have much time to get ready. I was about to get into the shower when I heard the kids walk out into the hall. They were talking a mile a minute and I could hear the excitement in their voices as they started down the stairs. Olivia followed behind them reminding them about all of her little rules. When the hallway fell silent, I went to take my shower. I knew Olivia would be waiting, so I didn't waste any time getting ready. Once I was dressed, I grabbed my phone and keys and started for Olivia's apartment. When I opened my door, Olivia was standing there. She was stunning. Her long, auburn brown hair fell loose around her shoulders, and she wore one of those little black dresses with a pair of black heels. Fuck. The woman was going to be the death of me. I had no idea how I was going to be able to keep my hands off of her, and the way she was looking at me like I was her next meal wasn't making it any easier.

"Hey," she said softly.

"Hey." I smiled. As she stepped inside my apartment, I asked, "Did the kids make it okay?"

"Yeah. They were really excited about it."

"They'll have fun," I tried to convince her.

"I think Charlie's hoping that a girl he likes is going to be there."

"That would definitely make the night more interesting," I chuckled. Damn. The small talk was killing me. I just wanted to reach out and grab her, carry her to the bedroom, and put an end to the tension that was building between us, but that would have to wait. I started for the door and asked, "You ready?"

"No."

I was surprised by her answer, so I turned around to face her. "No?"

"No," she answered again, more firmly this time. Her teeth nipped at her bottom lip as she stood staring at me. Finally, with her cheeks blushing red, she said, "I'd rather just stay here."

She didn't say the words. She didn't have to. Just one look at her and I knew exactly why she wanted to stay home. After a week of waiting, we were finally alone, and the last thing either of us wanted was to spend our night out surrounded by strangers. I dropped my keys on the table and said, "Staying here sounds good."

"Okay," she said nervously.

"Olivia," I growled as I took as step towards her.

"Yeah?"

"I noticed."

Her eyebrows furrowed as she tried to figure out what I was talking about. "Noticed what?"

"The cutoffs. The buttons on your uniform. All the excuses to put your hands on me. I noticed."

A sexy smile spread across her face as she said, "I don't know what you are talking about."

"You've been torturing me all week."

"The way you were acting, I didn't even think you were paying attention."

"I was. And just so you know ... you're going to pay for that shit."

Chapter 17
Olivia

He took a step towards me, but I didn't move. I couldn't. I knew what was coming. Hell, I'd asked for it, and he wanted it just as much as I did. I could see it in his eyes as they shimmered in the darkness, and my heart began to race with elation as he continued to move closer to me. It was happening. The moment that I'd envisioned so many times, and I was overcome with nerves, excitement, and desire all at the same time.

When he reached for me, I swallowed, holding my breath as I waited for him to lower his mouth to mine. Just before his lips touched mine, he paused. His gorgeous green eyes fell on me, searching for some kind of confirmation that I wanted this as much as he did, and when he found what he was looking for, his mouth crashed against my lips. My legs began to tremble as I was consumed with all of these feelings, these little sensations that had my body melting into his. I didn't question it. I didn't let my worries of inadequacies sneak into the back of my mind. Instead, I let myself go. I was there with him ... the place I was meant to be.

Clutch

The tips of his fingers trailed along my spine, and I arched towards him, seeking the heat of his touch. As he continued to kiss me, I could feel a fire burning deep inside me, smoldering as it spread through my body. It had started with just a spark, but I could feel it building, intensifying with every touch of his hand. He brought the tips of his fingers to the straps of my dress and gently brushed them off my shoulders. I shivered with anticipation as I felt the palm of his hand linger over my bare flesh. The satin dress slipped ever so slowly down my body, eventually puddling uselessly around my feet. He looked down at me, sending chills through my body as his eyes roamed over every inch of my exposed skin.

"So worth the wait," he muttered as he ran his rough, calloused finger along the edge of my black lace bra.

A rush of heat rolled against my skin as he stood there staring at me, appraising me. Everything about this man had my senses going completely haywire. I'd never wanted anything like I wanted him in that moment. Just looking at him made it hard to breathe, hard to think, and the way his eyes filled with lust when he looked at me only increased my need for him. I reached out, grasping the hem of his t-shirt, and I felt the muscles of his chest quiver as I my fingers brushed along his skin. Something about him lit me up from the inside, and just touching him made the fire inside me burn brighter and stronger, and I was having a hard time keeping it together. When I finally managed to pull the shirt over his head, I laid my hand on his heart, relieved to feel that his beat was fast and hard like mine. I wasn't the only one feeling this connection between us. Just like me, he'd felt every spark, every flicker of heat that surged through our bodies.

"Clutch," I whispered.

"Right here, baby. I've got you," he reassured me.

His lips brushed against mine, but not gently like before. Instead, it was hot, passionate, and demanding. I feared that I might lose myself in his touch, but I couldn't pull myself away. I wanted him too much, needed him too much. I moaned into his mouth, stealing the last of his restraint. I gasped when he lifted me up, cradling me close to his chest as he carried me over to the bed. He held me tightly, making me feel safe and secure in his arms. Seconds later, I was on my back and his body covered mine. His weight pressed me into the bed as his hands, rough and impatient, roamed over my body. Seconds later, my bra was freed from my body and thrown to the floor. His mouth closed over my breast, scraping his teeth across my sensitive flesh. My fingers tangled in his hair as he flicked his tongue against my nipple, sending goosebumps prickling across my skin. My breath caught as his hand slid between my legs. He ran his finger along the edge of my lace panties, trailing that vulnerable line between my thigh and center while his other hand cupped my breast, the rough pad of his thumb stroking across my nipple as he added fuel to the fire burning within me.

Impatient for more, I reached down, tugging at his belt, then lowered his jeans down his hips. I couldn't wait a moment longer. I needed to be taken. I needed to feel him inside of me. I looked up at him and pleaded, "Now."

He lifted off of me and reached for his jeans, searching for a condom. He was beautiful with his perfectly defined abs and his oh-so-pronounced V, and seeing him stand there in all of his naked glory had me swooning like some kind of nymphomaniac. When he caught me gawking at him, his eyes danced with mischief as he asked, "Like what you see, Sunshine?"

All I could muster was a brief nod and, "Mmm-hmm."

His smirk quickly faded as he looked down at me sprawled out on the bed, and then he said, "You're amazing, Olivia. Absolutely amazing."

Before I had time to respond, he was back on top of me, centering himself between my legs. He hovered over me, the heat of our breaths mingling between us until the anticipation became too much and his mouth crashed down around mine. His hand dove into my hair, grasping at the nape of my neck as he delved deeper into my mouth, our tongues twisting and tasting each other with all the passion and desire we'd kept bottled up since the first night we'd met. Without warning, his hands drifted down my thighs as he lowered my panties. Once they were gone, I wrapped my legs around him, taking him deep inside me. I instantly felt engulfed by him and froze, needing a minute to adjust to his size. After a brief moment, I placed my hands on his chest and slowly began to move, matching the rhythm of his heart as I rocked my hips against him.

Bliss. Pure bliss. Being with him was nothing like I'd ever experienced before. I had no idea it could be so good, and I wanted to savor the moment. I wanted to let myself feel every erotic sensation.

But Clutch had other plans. A deep growl vibrated through his chest as his pace quickened, becoming more demanding and intense with each shift of his hips. The muscles in my abdomen began to tighten and, without thinking, my legs drew up beside him. My hands curled around his back as I held on to him, bracing myself for the next wave of pleasure that crashed through my body. With one deep thrust, the fire ragged inside me, consuming every inch of me with heat as my orgasm tore through me. I was left shocked and shuddering from the explosion of pleasure, but he didn't stop. Not even close. He drove into me again and again until he found his own release, growling out like a satisfied bear as he lowered his body onto mine. I lay there limp beneath him as I listened to the rapid beating of his heart begin to slow and eventually return to a relaxed pace.

He eased off of me and rolled over on his side, pulling me close to him. Looking over to him, I finally got it. For the first time ever, I truly understood what all the hype was about. Smiling, I rested my head on his shoulder and whispered, "Fireworks."

"Fireworks?" he chuckled.

"Yep. I had no idea, but fireworks … they're good. Very, very good."

He cocked his head to the side and asked, "You gonna tell me about these fireworks?"

"Nope. All you need to know is that they're good."

"I guess I'll just have to take your word for it." He laughed at that. "You know, I promised Charlie that I'd take you for a night out on the town."

I curled up next to him, and as I ran my hand over his chest, I said, "This was way better than a night on the town."

"No doubt about that, but I should at least feed you. You hungry?"

"I could eat, but you're going to have to pry me out of this bed. I don't think I can move even if I wanted to."

He sat up on the bed. "Then, we'll get something delivered. Pizza or Chinese?"

"Ummm … Chinese. Some wontons would be great."

"Wontons it is." He got out of the bed. I didn't miss the opportunity to check out his perfect ass as he reached for the remote control and tossed it onto the bed. He gave me a knowing look as he said, "You find us something to watch while I call in our order."

"What do you want to watch?" I asked him as I curled up in the covers and turned on the TV.

"You've got the remote. You decide." He was still completely naked as he walked out of the room, and even though my body was still trembling from my cataclysmic orgasm, I was tempted to call him back to bed. Trying to distract myself, I started flipping through the channels, searching for something decent for us to watch, and finally settled on some romantic comedy. I could hear the rumble of his voice as he talked in the living room, followed by the slap of his bare feet against the hardwood floors as he walked back into the room.

He stopped at the foot of the bed and gave me a mischievous look before his hand dropped and took hold of the covers. He gave them a quick tug, pulling them completely off the bed.

"Hey! What are you doing?" I scolded as I quickly sat up and tried to reach for one of the blankets. Without answering, he lowered himself to the bed and started towards me like a panther after his prey. When he started trailing kisses along my leg, I giggled. "Clutch! What are you doing??"

A devilish smirk crossed his face. "You didn't think I was finished with you yet, did you?"

"It's been, like, five minutes. I thought it took time to build up ... you know ... *your resources* before you could do that again."

"My resources are just fine, Sunshine. Besides, it's time for a little payback for all the hell you put me through this week," he teased.

I started squirming beneath him. "What kind of

payback?"

Just before he kissed me, he lowered his mouth just inches above mine as he said, "The good kind."

There was one thing about Clutch: the man was true to his word. The payback was the good kind every single time. We never made it out of his room, and I couldn't have been happier. We made love, ate enough Chinese food for ten people, and watched movies. I loved being with him, and even though I was glad that the kids were coming home, I hated for the night to end. Spending the night in his arms made me realize just how much I wanted things to work out with him. It was such a huge turnaround from the day I'd first seen him. Back then, I thought that it'd be a mistake—a monumental, life-altering mistake—to get involved with him, but I couldn't have been more wrong. He was good to me and to the kids, and he made me happy. Happy wasn't something I ever expected to be again, but at that moment, I truly was. In fact, I couldn't remember a time when I was happier. I just wished my mother was there. I missed talking to her, telling her all of the crazy things that were going on in my life and listening to her words of wisdom about this or that. I knew she'd have plenty to say about my newfound relationship with Clutch, but she'd be able to see how happy I was. Even though she wasn't there to tell me herself, I already knew what she'd say. She'd smile and tell me to follow my heart, and that was exactly what I planned to do.

Chapter 18
Clutch

Fireworks. The minute Olivia said the word, I knew exactly what she meant. I'd felt them right along with her. Hell, I'd felt them every time we'd touched. The first time her lips met mine, it just about knocked me on my ass. I'd never felt anything like it before, and I couldn't get enough. Lucky for me, she felt the same way. We'd become quite the mischievous duo over the past couple of weeks, sneaking around like two fucking teenagers, only we weren't hiding from our parents; we were hiding from the kids. We'd made good use of our lunch breaks, and even managed to make up some pretty decent excuses to slip off and spend an hour or two alone after work. We thought we were being so fucking clever, but kids have a sixth sense about shit, and they knew something was up. I could see it in their eyes whenever we'd try to justify our reasons for being alone together.

"I'm going to go over and help Clutch fix his laptop. He thinks he's got a virus," Olivia told Charlie.

He raised an eyebrow and asked, "Virus, huh?

What kind of virus?"

She looked over at me, pleading with me to help, but I just stood there with a smirk on my face and said nothing, enjoying the show. Finally, she answered, "I don't know. That's why I'm going to go help him fix it."

He then turned to me and asked, "What's it doing?"

"Uh … I don't know. The screen went black or something," I mumbled.

"Sounds bad." He smiled. "Might need to get someone that actually knows how to turn on a computer to look at it."

Olivia rolled her eyes at him. "I know a lot about computers, smart one. I can fix his laptop."

"Uh huh. Whatever you say, Sis. Next time, just say you're going over to Clutch's place. You don't have to come up with some lame excuse."

"It's not—" Olivia started.

"Liv, let's just go," I told her as I took her hand and led her next door. "We'll be back. Keep the door locked."

It was exhausting trying to outsmart those two kids, and I was actually relieved when Charlie called us on our shit. Olivia tried her best to convince herself that her brother didn't know what we were up to, and I wasn't going to be the one that broke the news to her.

As soon as I closed the door behind us, she asked, "Do you think he knows we're fooling around?"

I walked over to her, pinning her hot little body

against the wall, and as I lowered my mouth down to hers, I whispered, "No way to know for sure unless you ask him."

Before I had a chance to kiss her, she screeched, "Ask him? I can't ask him!"

"Then, leave it," I answered, and before she had a chance to respond, I pressed my lips against hers, stealing her next thought.

That's all it took. She let go of her worries about the kids and wrapped her arms around my neck, immediately filling the room with her little moans and whimpers. My hands drifted down to her thighs, lowering her shorts and lace panties down her long, lean legs. My dick was straining against my jeans as I began to unbuckle them and let them fall to the floor. In a frenzy of need, I lifted her up and pressed her back against the wall as she wrapped her legs around my waist. Just watching the look on her face as I slammed my cock deep inside her made me come undone. I quickened my pace, pounding into her again and again, each thrust more demanding than the last.

She ground her hips against mine, matching my relentless rhythm as she whimpered, "More."

Fuck. My girl wanted more, and that's just what I gave her. Her grip on my shoulders tightened as I tilted her hips, driving deeper and harder with every move. I felt her clamp down around my cock, letting me know that her climax was approaching. I came seconds after her body fell limp in my arms. I held her close as I told her, "You're mine, Olivia Turner. I'm never letting you go."

With a satisfied smile spreading across her face, she asked, "Are you mine, too? Does it work both ways?"

"Absolutely," I agreed as I carried her over to the sofa.

"You're pretty awesome. You know that, right?"

I laughed as I said, "Yeah ... I have my moments."

She rested her head on my shoulder, and as I ran my fingers through her hair, she softly said, "You have lots of moments. And you should know, I love them all. And I love you, too."

Never before had words sounded so sweet, and hearing them from her the first time had me wanting to make love to her all over again. My world stood still as I turned to face her and said, "I love you, too, Sunshine."

She pressed her lips to mine, and we completely became lost in the moment. Just before we had a chance to get carried away, we both heard Charlie and Hadley arguing next door. With a growl, Olivia got up. As she got dressed, she pouted. "Duty calls."

She kissed me one last time and headed for the door. Our moments alone were short, but they were enough. I savored every minute I could have with her. Being with her was the only thing that kept me going when things went to shit at the garage. I'd been going in early every day trying to get ahead, but the weekend was just around the corner and I hadn't made the progress I'd hoped to make. When all the guys started packing up for the night, I decided I'd follow them out. There was nothing on that engine that couldn't wait until tomorrow, and I needed to touch base with Big Mike.

As soon as I got out to my bike, I gave him a call and was immediately concerned about what he'd found. Turned out that Hanson made a few bad investments. He'd lost a shit load of money, and the pressure was on him to make a quick turnaround. He was desperate, and desperate men do desperate things. Mike was following a lead on one of the men Hanson was dealing with and promised to get back with me when he found out more. After talking to him, I got on my bike and headed home. I'd barely walked into my apartment when I heard a knock at my door. I looked over at the clock and, seeing that it was before seven, I knew it wasn't Olivia. We'd made plans to go riding over the weekend, so she'd been working late all week trying to get in a few extra hours so she could take a day off. When I opened the door, I was surprised to find Charlie standing there waiting for me.

He stepped into the apartment and said, "You know Sam? The guy that Livie has been feeding at the diner?"

"Yeah?"

"I found out today at school who beat him up," he told me with worry in his voice.

When he didn't continue, I prodded him. "You gonna tell me who it was?"

"His name is Isaac Puckett. He's a real douchebag. He's always screwing around with folks and acting like he is such a badass. He's always running his damn mouth about something. Everybody at school hates him, except for a couple of guys who follow him around like he's some kind of god or something. They do whatever he tells them to do."

"Sounds like a real winner. How do you know it was him?"

"I usually just stay away from him and his friends, but I overheard them talking in the locker room after PE today. Puckett was bragging about how he and a couple of his friends beat up some homeless guy, and even mentioned using a crowbar on him. He started getting all hyped up and said they should go try and find him tonight so they could beat the shit out of him again. They even mentioned coming by the diner to find him."

"Shit. How old is this kid?"

"Pretty sure he failed a couple of times. Somebody said he was like nineteen or something, but he's just a junior," he explained.

"Any idea where I might find this kid?"

"He'll be at the weight room for another hour or two. The coach assigned him an extra hour of weightlifting for being late to practice, so he told his crew to meet him at the park around eight tonight."

"You happen to have a picture of this guy?"

"No, but you don't need one. He's almost six-two, but he's pretty slim. Might weigh a hundred and seventy-five pounds. He's got black hair with dreads and he always wears a big diamond earring in his ear. And he drives an old beat-up green Jeep."

"Little tyke, huh?"

"He's tall, but a pussy without his friends around. He'll be the only one at the weight room tonight. Are you going after him?"

"Might have a little chat with him," I admitted.

"Can I go with you?"

"Not a chance, man. Your sister would kill us both, but I do need you to do me a favor. Go get the keys to Olivia's car while I change clothes."

"Okay." A look of disappointment crossed his face as he headed for the door, and before he walked out, he said, "Just make sure he doesn't hurt Sam again. I'd hate for anything to happen to him."

"You can count on that."

After I made a quick stop for necessities, I made it to the school around seven-thirty. Just like Charlie had said, Puckett's Jeep was the only one in the lot. I took care of the sad excuse of a security camera and waited for my young friend to come out of the weight room. I stood behind the door, and when he finally stepped out, I placed the barrel of my gun against the back of his head and pulled back the hammer Even though he was just a kid, he knew the familiar click of a cocking gun. He stood there frozen like a statue.

"We are going to take a little ride, Puckett. And then you and me are going to have a little chat. You got that?" When he nodded, I said, "Go over to the car and place your hands on the trunk."

He did as he was told, and to my surprise, he didn't resist when I pulled his hands behind his back. To my benefit, he was too scared to move, much less scream out for help. After I'd zip-tied his hands together, I turned him around to face me. It was hard to believe this guy was still in high school. He looked like he was in his mid-twenties with his dreads and thick goatee. But even though he was a big dude, he was still terrified out of his mind. He tried his best to swallow his fear as he stood there looking at me, but I could tell by the way his bottom lip was trembling that he was freaking out. He looked down at me and asked, "What you want, man?"

"You'll see soon enough. Get your ass in the car," I ordered as I popped the trunk open.

He managed to keep up his brave front until he spotted the concrete cinder block and three-quarter-inch chain sitting next to the spare tire in the bottom of the trunk. Seeing them only terrified him more, spurring him to put up a fight. He bucked against me, trying to break free from my hold, but with one good jab into his rib cage, he buckled. I gave him a good shove, forcing him into the trunk.

Before I slammed it shut, he whimpered, "Please let me go, man. I didn't do nothing."

"That's where we disagree, Puckett. You've done plenty, and now you're going to pay for it," I told him as I shut the trunk.

As I got in the car, I heard him kicking his feet against the trunk. Ignoring him, I started the car and drove out of the parking lot. I pulled up beside the bank of the Mississippi River and parked the car. I got out and opened the trunk. His eyes widened as he watched me grab the cinder block and chain and place it on the ground. I took a hold of his arm and started pulling him out of the car.

As soon as his feet hit the ground, he asked, "Why are you doing this? I already told you I didn't do nothing, man."

Without answering him, I started wrapping the thick chain around his feet, then worked my way up to his arms and waist. The entire time, he was pleading with me to stop, begging with everything he had for me to let him go. I ignored him. When I was finished wrapping the chain around his body, I looped the remaining length around the cinder block and secured it with a lock. I shoved the key in his front pocket and gave him a quick push, forcing him against the car.

"Word on the street is you're a real asshole. I don't have much patience for assholes, Puckett. As a matter of fact, I have *no* patience whatsoever for assholes, especially stupid, fucking assholes like you. So, I tell you what I'm going to do. I'm going to drag your sorry ass over to that river and watch your skinny little butt sink to the bottom."

"I ain't never did nothing to nobody, man. I just do my thing and leave folks alone," he said defensively. I reached for his arm, and when I gave him an angry tug, he yelped, "Wait! I've got some money. It ain't much, but you can have it. Just give me some time and I'll get you some more. Whatever you want, just let me go," he pleaded.

"What I want...? That's a good place to start," I told him as I reared back my fist and punched him in the gut. He bent over with a pitiful groan as I said, "See, I got this friend. He's a real decent guy, Puckett. Unlike you, he minds his own fucking business. Stays out of trouble. Doesn't fuck with people just to be fucking with them. Turns out, he had a run-in with you and a couple of your buddies the other night. You decided to use him as a punching bag, and that was a mistake, Puckett. A big fucking mistake," I told him as I punched him again.

He groaned as he stuttered, "I'm s-sorry. I didn't ... know."

"Of course you didn't know he was my friend. How could you know that? You'd have to be some kind of genius to know that, but we both know you're just a stupid asshole," I told him as I slammed my fist against his jaw.

"I said I was sorry," he cried as blood trickled from the corner of his mouth. "Please ... just stop."

I hit him again, causing his eye to immediately begin to swell. "Did you stop? No, I don't think you did. As a matter of fact, you even used a crowbar to wail on him, and you were bragging about it at school. You were making plans to do it again. Isn't that right, Puckett? You were going to do that shit again. You had no intention of stopping."

"I was just ... fucking around, man," he stammered. "I wasn't gonna—"

"You've got a bad habit of running your fucking mouth, Puckett. No one likes an asshole who runs his fucking mouth all the time. And no one likes an asshole who's always fucking around with folks ... especially me, Puckett. I can't stand that shit. There's nothing worse, but all that's going to stop. Isn't that right?"

"Uh huh," he mumbled.

I yanked him up and started dragging him towards the water. When we reached the bank, I said, "I didn't hear you, Puckett."

"I'll stop running my fucking mouth," he shouted.

"And?"

"I won't fuck with anyone ever again. Just please."

"You've got one shot here, asshole. You or your friends make one wrong move, there won't be any more second chances. Next time, your sorry ass will be at the bottom of this river, and no one will ever find you. Is that understood?"

"Yes, sir. I understand."

With the chains still wrapped around his feet, I pulled him back to the car and tossed him back into the trunk. I drove back to the school, and once I had pulled up next to Puckett's Jeep, I got out and walked over to the trunk. I opened it to find Puckett staring back at me with a worried look on his face. He knew I wasn't done with him. I reached for him, yanking him and the cinder block out of the trunk, and pulled him over to the front of his Jeep. I lifted him up, sitting him on the hood, then I pulled a permanent marker out of my back pocket and wrote, "I'm an asshole" on his forehead.

I took a step closer and got up in his face as I said, "Don't make me come back here, Puckett. Walk a straight line, or you'll be done."

"You gonna leave me here like this?" he asked as he tried to move but couldn't.

"Yeah. I am," I told him as I started walking towards my car. "Remember what I said, Puckett."

As I started the engine, I could hear him pleading with me to let him go, but I just ignored him and drove out of the parking lot. I didn't bother telling Charlie about my night with Puckett. I knew he'd find out as soon as he got to school. Sure enough, the next day I overheard him telling Olivia all about it. He was laughing as he told her about the kids finding him bound to the hood of his car. Apparently, Puckett's cronies were nowhere to be found, and it took several hours before anyone released him from his restraints. Charlie seemed relieved when he told her that there was an immediate change in Puckett's attitude, letting me know that my time with him had been well spent. Sometimes, all it takes is a little push to get a person back on the right track.

Chapter 19
Olivia

When Clutch told me that he was going to take me for a ride on his bike, I was intrigued, but hesitant. I'd always been interested in trying it out, but I'd heard on more than one occasion that motorcycles were dangerous. I knew I'd be safe with Clutch, so I let go of my reservations and agreed to give it a whirl. When he pulled up to the curb to pick me up, my heart skipped a beat. Seeing him on his bike looking all kinds of sexy in his faded jeans and leather jacket had my senses going into overload. I took a deep breath and tried to ignore my libido as I walked over to him. I'd worn jeans and boots like he'd told me and was feeling pretty confident until he handed me the helmet. I fiddled with it, but I had no idea how to strap the darn thing on. I didn't miss the smirk on Clutch's face as he watched me, and I was just about to get flustered when he pulled me over to him.

"Come here, Sunshine," he told me as he took the strap from my hand. "You loop it through the bottom ring and then back through the first."

"Easy enough," I told him as he snapped it to the side.

"You're all set. Now hop on," he ordered.

"Wait … aren't you going to tell me what to do?" I squealed.

He smiled. "You get on and ride. That's about it."

"Come on, Clutch. There's more to it than that. Do I lean into the turn or away from the turn? And where do I put my feet? And how do I keep myself from falling off the darn thing??"

"Liv, get on the bike." He smirked. "I'm going to show you everything you need to know. It's just easier when you're on the bike."

"Okay," I huffed as I hiked my leg up and over the seat, quickly situating myself behind him. I put my feet on the foot pegs and my hands on his hips, then waited for him to tell me wait to do next.

"You've already got the hard part down," he teased. "And as far as the turns go, just go with what feels right or lean against the backrest."

"And what about falling off?"

"You're not going to fall off, Liv. Just relax and enjoy the ride," he assured me as he started the engine.

Seconds later, we were headed out onto the main road, zipping through traffic like it was something we'd done a hundred times, only we hadn't ridden a hundred times, and I was a nervous wreck. My heart was pounding against my chest and my palms were all sweaty. I thought my first ride with him would be exhilarating, being all snuggled up close to him as I felt the wind in my face and the sun against my skin, but I was too lost in my little freak-out to even enjoy it. I was worried that I was holding on too tight or not tight enough, and I kept wondering whether I should lean into the curves with him or press my back against the seat like he'd suggested. And every time we stopped at a light, I thought I was getting a small reprieve, but as soon as the light turned green, he'd shoot out into traffic, lunging me against his back.

I felt his chest vibrate with laughter as he shouted, "You're doing great, Sunshine. Just relax."

"I am relaxed," I lied.

"Liv," he scolded. "I'm not going to let anything happen to you. Just take a deep breath and let go."

Realizing he was right, I tried my best to stop worrying so much. I took a deep breath and let go of the tension I'd been carrying for the past hour and finally started to enjoy the ride. In no time, I'd gotten the hang of the turns and felt like I actually knew what the hell I was doing. We rode for several hours. I marveled at how the sunlight danced across the Mississippi River as we crossed over the Arkansas bridge. It was amazing, seeing things from the perspective of a motorcycle. Everything seemed closer and more defined, and with the added excitement of being pressed against Clutch, I couldn't have enjoyed it more. Unfortunately, our moment in the sun was about to be over … in more ways than we realized.

As the sun was about to set, we headed back to the apartment. Louise had been checking on the kids while we were gone, and it was almost time for her to leave the diner when we got there. We got off the bike, and I was just about to go inside to thank her when Sam called out to me.

"Hazel!" There was a look of panic on his face as he rushed over to us and said, "Y'all need to come around back … now."

"What's going on?" Clutch asked him.

"I think you've got trouble coming," he answered as he turned and started towards the back alley.

"What kind of trouble?" I asked.

He shrugged and said, "I don't know. Only you have the answer to that."

When we finally made it down the long, dingy alley, Clutch and I both were surprised to find a large man lying face down in the dirt with his hands bound behind his back. I walked over to him and saw that he had blood trickling from the back of his head and he was completely knocked out. He was fairly short, or at least he looked shorter than me, and he had blondish gray hair and wore a dress shirt with a pair of khakis. I didn't recognize him, so I turned to Sam and asked, "Who is he?"

"No idea. Never seen the guy before, but I heard him talking on his phone, and when he mentioned a waitress at the diner and the two kids, I started paying attention. He was telling someone about the hours you were working and all about your apartment upstairs. He even told them where the kids were going to school. It sounded like whoever he was talking to was on his way here."

"Fuck," Clutch growled.

"I didn't like the sound of it, so I knocked the guy out. He never saw me coming. I plowed him in the back of the head, and he dropped like a two-ton shit house."

"You did good, brother," Clutch told him as he took out his phone and started calling someone.

"What are you going to do?" I asked him. "We need to call the police!"

"No. No police, Liv. Just give me a minute. Gotta call Cyrus." Seconds later, he started speaking into his phone, "Hey, man. We got trouble. Need you to bring a cage over to the diner. I'll explain more when you get here. Bring Blaze and one of the other guys with you." There was a brief pause. "Thanks, brother."

"Shouldn't we call Detective Brakeman?"

"No, Liv. We don't know how this guy found you, and until I get some answers, we trust no one outside of the club." Clutch growled. "I need you to get upstairs and get you and the kids packed up. Just get the necessities."

"Okay." I looked over at the man lying on the ground and asked, "What about him?"

"Don't worry about him. I'll handle it."

"Okay," I said softly.

Clutch reached out and pulled me into his arms as

he said, "I've got you, Sunshine. I'm not going to let anything happen to you or to those kids, but I'm going to need you to trust me. You may not understand or even like how this is all going to play out, but it's the best way to make sure that you and the kids are safe."

"I'm scared," I whispered.

He held me tight. "I know, baby, but it's going to be okay. Now, I need you to get upstairs and get packed up."

I nodded and then rushed upstairs. When I opened the door, Charlie was sitting on the couch watching TV and totally unaware that I was about to pull the rug out from underneath him. As soon as he looked up and saw the expression on my face, he asked, "What's wrong?"

"I ... I don't know how to say this without freaking you out, but—"

He sat up and faced me. "Just spit it out, Livie."

"They found us. We've got to pack up and get out of here ... now."

"Holy shit. Are you sure?"

"Yeah, I'm sure." I knew that he'd started to really like being in Memphis and he'd made a lot of new friends, and I hated that he had to leave it all behind again. "I'm sorry, buddy."

"Where are we gonna go?"

"I don't know. Clutch just told me to pack us up and he's taking care of the rest. And, Charlie ... we need to be careful how we tell Hadley. I don't want to scare her."

"I already heard," she whispered.

I turned around and found her standing in the hallway with tears trickling down her face. I rushed over to her and wrapped my arms around her, hugging her tightly as I promised, "We're going to be okay, sweetheart. We just need to get our things and get downstairs. Clutch is waiting for us."

"So ... Clutch is going to help us?" she asked.

"Yeah, he is. He'll do whatever it takes to keep us safe. You know that," I assured her.

She stepped back and headed for her room as she said, "Let's get to packing, then."

My little sister was a brave one, and I couldn't have been more proud. It didn't take us long to pack, and with our hands piled high with everything we could shove in our duffle bags, we met Clutch downstairs. When I looked around, I saw that the stranger was nowhere to be found, and Clutch was talking to Blaze. I'd only met him once, but Clutch talked about him all the time. I knew he thought a lot of him, so I wasn't surprised that he'd asked him to come. When we walked up, Clutch told Charlie, "You and Hadley put the bags in the back of the black SUV while I talk to your sister for a minute."

Once they were gone, I asked, "Where are you taking us?"

"I'm not taking you, Liv. Blaze and T-Bone are going to get you to Casper, Wyoming where you're going to meet up with Smokey. From there, Smokey and Maverick will get you back to my clubhouse in Washington. It's going to take a couple of days, but once you get there, you'll be safe. They'll take care of you until I can get there," he explained.

"What do you mean you aren't going?"

He took a step closer and placed his hands on my shoulders as he said, "I've got to stay here so I can take care of all of this. It's the only way."

"Why can't I just take my car? Why do we have to go in that SUV?" I asked.

"They may know your car. Don't want them to be able to track you, and besides … it's better if they still think you are here."

"Clutch, this is all just too much. What are your brothers going to think when I just show up at your clubhouse with two kids?"

"I meant it when I said you are mine. I claimed you, Liv, in every way that matters. My brothers know that. They'll treat you like family and will do whatever needs to be done to make sure you are safe and comfortable. And I'll be there as soon as I can."

I could see that he wanted me to go along with his plan, but I was scared out of my mind. I wanted him to be with me and the kids, not dealing with the psycho who killed my parents. If something happened to him, I wouldn't be able to live with myself. I loved him, so I pleaded, "Please come with us, Clutch. I don't want to leave here without you."

"I know that, and if I could go with you, I would.

But I can't be in two places at once, and I've gotta be here to see this thing through. I love you and I love those kids, and I wouldn't do this if I didn't think it was the best way to protect you, Liv."

"What about you? Who's going to keep you safe?" I asked, but before he responded, I got my answer. Eight motorcycles came barreling into the parking lot with men wearing the same kind of leather jacket that Clutch was always wearing. In any other situation, I would've been intimidated by the stream of burly bikers approaching us, but these men were there to help Clutch … to help us … and it meant the world to me.

The biggest one of the bunch came up to Clutch and asked, "Where's her apartment?"

"It's upstairs. The first one on the left," Clutch answered. When the man started for the door, Clutch called out, "Hey, Runt. Here are the keys." Clutch tossed him my keys, and then several of the men followed him, carrying a variety of boxes and tools.

"What are they going to do?" I asked.

"Just setting up surveillance," Gus answered as he walked up behind us. "We're gonna take care of all of this for you, doll. You just get those kids to Washington safe and sound and leave the rest to us."

I knew he was the president of the club and not a man to be questioned, but I had to ask, "Why are you doing all of this?"

Clutch looked at me and answered for him by saying, "I already told you, Liv. When you're part of the club, you're family, and our family looks after their own. You and those kids are my family now, so the club is going to do whatever it takes to keep you all safe," he explained. "It's just how it works."

I turned to Gus and said, "Thank you."

"No need for thanks, doll. It's what we do. Now, it's time for you to get on the road. You've got a long drive ahead," Gus replied.

Clutch followed me over to the SUV, and once I'd placed my bags in the trunk, he slipped his hands around my waist, pulling me over to him. He pressed his lips against mine, kissing me softly, before he said, "Keep your eyes open. Blaze and T-Bone will make sure you get there without any problems, but if you need me, I'm just a phone call away."

"I love you, Shaggy Thomas. No matter what happens, don't forget that," I told him.

"I love you, too, Olivia. Now get your ass in that truck," he told me as he gave my rear a quick pop. "I'll call you in a couple of hours to check on you."

I got in the passenger side of the SUV and Blaze drove us out onto the main road. I tried my best to hide my nerves as I told the kids, "I guess we're in for a little adventure."

"Where are we going?" Hadley asked.

"We're headed to Washington. We're going to Clutch's clubhouse to stay for a few days."

"The clubhouse? That will be so cool," Charlie grinned.

I wish I could've been as optimistic as my younger brother, but I was a mess. I couldn't believe all of this was happening. It was all so surreal. We'd come so far since the day we packed up our things and moved from Boston. It wasn't easy ... none of it. The kids and I struggled every day trying to accept the fact that our parents were gone, but we were getting there. Each day got a little easier, and I was actually feeling good about things, especially when Clutch came into the picture. I was starting to believe that we could truly have a normal life. I couldn't have been more wrong. I felt like my world had been rocked on its axis all over again, and I knew the kids were feeling the same way.

My mind was bombarded with a whirlwind of uncertainty, but there was one thing I knew for sure: Clutch would see us through the storm. He had to, because without him, we'd have no second chance.

Chapter 20
Clutch

So much had changed over the past few months, making me realize that when I decided to take a break from the club, I wasn't walking away from what I really wanted; I was walking towards it.

I'd found the life I'd always wanted with Olivia, and watching her pull out of the parking lot with Charlie and Hadley was one of the hardest things I've ever done. Everything I cared about was in that car, and even though I wanted to keep them close, I knew sending them to the club was the only way to ensure their safety. I couldn't risk anything happening to them, even if that meant being away from them. I just had to remind myself that the sooner I dealt with the men who were after Olivia and the kids, the sooner I'd be able to get back to them, so I got on my bike and followed Gus back to the clubhouse.

By the time we got there, their club's enforcer, Bic, had already taken the fucker to the back warehouse. Apparently, Bic had gotten his road name because of his fascination with razor blades, which came in handy when he needed to extract information. Knowing I was eager, Gus led me straight to the back. When we walked in, the first thing I noticed was the room was nothing like ours. This room reminded me of an operating room with its strange smell and assortment of needles and blades lined along the butcher block counter. Everything about it was vastly different from the room we had back at home. Stitch, our club enforcer, had a more recognizable assortment of tools he used to work on our enemies. When I stepped further into the room, I spotted a man I figured was Bic sitting in a chair smoking a cigarette. He had a long burly beard and was wearing a white wife-beater with a pair of light blue scrubs. He seemed completely relaxed while our guy was bound to an old gurney, blubbering and crying under his breath. I was surprised to find that, other than the bump on his head, he didn't have a mark on him.

I walked over to Bic and asked, "Something holding you up?"

"Yeah, you," he grumbled. "Figured you'd want to be here for the show. Ask the questions you wanted to ask."

"Appreciate that, brother. Let's get this thing started," I told him.

He got up from his seat and, as soon as he started walking over to his table of tools, our guy started pleading, "Please ... there must be some misunderstanding here."

Bic ignored him as he walked over to his table and

picked up a long, pointed blade and, without speaking, he took the blade and used it to cut away the man's shirt, exposing the bare skin of his chest, causing him to come completely undone.

"Please! I don't know anything," he wailed.

"Now, I have a hard time believing that," Bic snickered, "but we'll find out soon enough."

He took the sharp end of the blade and raked it across the man's collarbone, causing a deep gash down to the bone. Then, with a gleam in his eye, Bic picked up a bottle of liquid and slowly poured it into the cut. An explosion of screams roared through the room as the man writhed beneath his restraints. A familiar aroma of bleach filled the room as he continued to cry out in pain, and I had no doubt that it hurt like a motherfucker.

When the guy finally stopped screaming, I approached the table and asked, "What's your name, asshole?"

"Rick … Michaels," he stammered.

"What do you know about Olivia Turner?" I pushed.

"I was hired … to find … her … and her brother and sister."

"Who hired you?" Bic asked.

With his eyes glued to the bottle of bleach Bic was still holding in his hand, Rick answered, "I don't know. He didn't give me his name … just a phone number." When Bic tilted the bottle over his chest, he squealed, "I swear! He didn't give me a name, but the guy was loaded. Paid me a hundred grand to start looking, and promised another hundred when I located them. Even sent an extra ten grand to cover my traveling expenses."

I could tell he was being honest about not knowing the man's name, but that didn't stop Bic from slicing him once again. He took the bottle in his hand as he asked, "What's the number?"

Pure panic washed over him as he cried out, "It's in my phone listed under 'Payday'. You can see for yourself. Just get my phone and look."

"What did you tell him about her?" I growled.

"Just what I knew … where she was living and where she worked. And I also told him where the kids were going to school."

"What else?" I shouted.

"I gave him the addresses and that's it. It was all I was paid to do!"

"How did you get your money?" Bic asked.

"He sent it straight to my bank account. I never even laid eyes on the guy," he confessed.

"Gonna need more than that, Rick," Bic warned.

He quickly added, "My account information is in my wallet. Maybe you can find out something from that. I tried to find it myself, but just kept finding dead ends."

I took a step closer. "What did you tell him about me and the club?"

"I didn't say anything about you, I swear. Didn't see any reason to. He was only concerned with the girl and the siblings."

"How did you find them?"

"You know how stupid kids are, always posting shit on all their social media sites. I used my facial recognition software. It took some time, but I finally got a hit when some kid posted a bunch of pictures of the sister and one of her friends doing some project at school."

"Something's not adding up here, Rick," Bic told him as he took the blade in his hand and carved another deep line down his chest, filling the room with gut-wrenching screams once again. When Rick settled down, Bic continued, "Seems you're pretty fucking good at that computer shit. Guy like you wouldn't have a problem finding out who deposited all that money into your account."

He reached for the bottle, and before Rick could answer, he covered his chest with the liquid, causing him to bellow out and squirm like a worm in hot ashes. When he started to pour it once again, Rick howled, "I never even tried to find him. Didn't give a fuck who the guy was. I just needed the cash!"

Gus walked over to me and said, "We'll get Crow to see what he can find out using the account information, but before we move forward, you need to be thinking about how you want this thing to play out. I think this guy might turn out to be useful."

"Whatcha got in mind?"

"Use the fucker as bait. Have him make a call or two to lure your guy in so we can get him exactly where you want," Gus suggested.

"I'll do whatever you want," Rick cried. "I got the number. I can call him anytime. Just please stop with the torture."

Bic stepped over to him, grabbing a handful of his hair as he placed the blade at his throat and growled, "You make one wrong move, say one wrong word, and you'll be right back in this spot, Little Ricky. And I'll spend hours slicing and dicing every fucking inch of you. You got that?"

"I get it. I get it. Like I said, I'll do whatever you guys tell me to," he promised.

Gus turned to Bic and said, "Lock him up out back until we need him."

"On it," he answered.

"Thanks, brother," I told him.

After we collected Rick's phone and wallet, I followed Gus back into the clubhouse and down the long hall to Crow's room. He tapped on the door, and as soon as Crow stuck his head out, Gus said, "Need your help with something, brother."

"Whatcha got?" he asked

"Need you to do a search on a deposit made to this account a few weeks ago. See if you can find out who made the deposit. Also got a phone number. Need anything you can find, and make it fast. No time to waste," Gus ordered.

"Give me an hour," he replied as he took the phone and account information from Gus. "I'll see what I can find."

Gus and I spent the next hour discussing the best way to handle the situation with Rick and the man who paid him to find Olivia and the kids. There was no doubt that Rick would lead us to the man who'd been pursuing them since the night their parents were killed. My blood boiled when I thought about the hell he'd put them through over the past few months. Olivia had busted her ass trying to protect those kids and give them a semblance of a normal life, and I'd be damned if this motherfucker was going to come in and take that away from them. He'd killed their parents, and if he thought he was going to do the same to them, he had another thing coming: me.

Chapter 21
Olivia

One mile marker blurred into the next as Blaze continued down the interstate. He was quiet, which was good. My mind was in a complete fog, and I just didn't have it in me to have some idle conversation with him. I was too lost in my own thoughts. My mind was bombarded with memories of the night my parents were killed and how scared we all were when we had to pack up what little we could and leave so much behind. I'd never been so scared and heartbroken, and the more I thought about it, I realized I'd never really had the time to mourn my parents' death. There was no time; I was too busy trying to survive and provide some kind of normal life for my brother and sister. I tried so hard, but I had no idea what I was doing. I didn't know how to be a parent, much less be a mother and a father to two children in the crazy circumstances we were living in, but I was figuring it out. When Clutch came into our lives with his sexy little smirk and leather jacket, I fought the pull I felt towards him. I fought it with everything I had. I thought he was trouble, and I didn't need a man like that in my life. I couldn't have been more wrong. With him at our side, we'd found a way to get through the chaos, and we were doing pretty well until Sam found that man in the alley. I couldn't help but wonder what would have happened if Sam hadn't overheard him talking about us. Everything we'd done would have all been in vain if he hadn't been there.

My stomach was in knots as I glanced back in the rearview mirror to see if T-Bone was still there. Just like every time I'd looked before, he was trailing close behind us. It was almost two in the morning before Blaze found us a motel and got us a couple of rooms. I grabbed our bags and led the kids up to our room. They looked like little zombies as they crawled into their beds, and within minutes, they were both sound asleep. Once I'd taken a long, hot shower, I curled up next to Hadley and closed my eyes, quickly giving in to my own exhaustion.

Unfortunately, it was short-lived. After only a few hours of sleep, I was jolted awake by a terrible nightmare. When I couldn't shake off the eerie feeling I'd gotten from the dream, I got out of bed and grabbed my jacket. As soon as I stepped outside, the chill of the early morning air snapped me out of my fog. It was still fairly dark and I was surprised to find Blaze standing out by the SUV smoking a cigarette.

I walked over to him and, seeing that he was fully dressed, I asked, "Couldn't sleep?"

"I got a few hours in." He yawned. "Enough to get

me by. What are you doing up so early?"

"Had a bad dream. Thought I'd come out for a little fresh air."

His eyebrows furrowed with concern as he said, "We've got a long drive ahead, Olivia. You need to get some sleep."

"I will in a second. Just need a minute to clear my head." I watched as he flicked his cigarette butt across the lot, then immediately lit another one and took a long drag. As the smoke billowed from his lips, I asked, "How's your son? I ... hope you don't mind me asking. I just remember Clutch telling me that he was worried about him," I explained.

He brought his cigarette up to his mouth and took a long drag before he said, "Nah, I don't mind ya asking. Kevin's doing alright. He was pretty sick there for a while, but he's doing better now."

"Sounds like a tough kid." I smiled. "How old is he?"

"He's six. Gonna be seven in a couple of weeks. The kid's growing so fast I can hardly keep up with him, but I wouldn't have it any other way."

"I bet he keeps you on your toes," I laughed.

"No doubt about that. He's always getting into something or another. Lately, his new kick is to get me to quit smoking. Always hiding my cigarettes and giving me hell every time he catches me with a cigarette in my hand. He's persistent, I'll give him that."

"Might be easier to just stop smoking."

"Yeah, you're probably right. Should've never started in the first place," he said as he tossed his cigarette to the ground. He nodded his head towards our hotel room and asked, "How are the kids taking all this?"

"They're scared, but this time it's different. This time they have Clutch."

"He's a good guy. He'll do right by them and by you. Just hang in there. He'll see you through all of this."

"God, I hope so. I can't go through all of this again."

"You won't have to. Clutch and the club will make sure of it," he assured me. "Now go get another hour of sleep. We need to get back on the road soon."

"Okay," I told him as I turned and started walking towards our room. I'd only taken a few steps when I turned to him and said, "Thanks for keeping an eye on us, Blaze. It means a lot to me."

He smiled and said, "Glad to do it."

As soon as I got to the room, I crawled back into bed and, after a few minutes of tossing and turning, I finally managed to fall back asleep. It felt like I'd just closed my eyes when I heard a banging on the door followed by T-Bone yelling, "Rise and shine, sleepyheads. We're rolling out in ten!"

Charlie groaned as he rolled over to face me. He rubbed his eyes. "Crap … What time is it?"

I looked at my watch. "It's almost eight." I tossed

back the covers. "Come on, guys. Get up. We need to get moving. I don't want to make them wait."

They both groaned as they pulled themselves out of bed. Once they were dressed, we met Blaze and T-Bone out in the parking lot. With a grumpy look on her face, Hadley walked over to T-Bone and said, "I'm hungry."

Laughing, he told her, "I feel ya, kid. Let's go grab some breakfast before we head out. How about some pancakes?"

"Anything is fine," I answered for her.

Blaze got in the SUV and said, "It'll be a while before we stop again. Might as well get something decent to eat before we go."

We followed T-Bone over to a small diner across the street, and once we were inside and sitting at a table, we each ordered a big breakfast and coffee. The kids were talking back and forth amongst themselves and seemed to be doing okay considering everything that was going on. I wish I could say the same for myself. I was tired, but wound up with nerves at the same time. Blaze must have noticed that I was tense, because he asked, "You doing alright?"

"I've been better, but I'll be okay. Just a little overwhelmed."

T-Bone leaned towards me and said, "My ma' used to tell me that sometimes you gotta go through hell before you get to the good stuff. You and those kids have good stuff coming, Olivia. You just gotta see this thing through."

"I'm trying. It's just a lot."

Blaze laid his hand on mine and gave it a light squeeze. "I'm right there with you. Seems like there will never be an end to all the bullshit, but the end is there. We'll get to the good. Knowing that is the only thing that keeps me going."

I smiled and said, "You're right. We'll get there."

The waitress placed our food on the table, and just before Hadley took her first bite, she looked over to T-Bone. "Are you really bald or do you shave your head?"

"Hadley!" I scolded.

T-Bone chuckled. "Because I want to."

I shook my head in embarrassment. "I'm sorry, T-Bone. Hadley's filter hasn't kicked in yet."

"I was just asking. I didn't mean anything by it," Hadley said defensively. She looked back over to T-Bone and continued, "So you shave it? Like every day?"

"Nah, just when I need to," he answered as he took a big bite of eggs. "Every couple of days I have to mow it down."

I looked over to Hadley and gave her a warning look, letting her know that it was time to end her line of questioning, but she didn't take the hint. Instead she asked, "Do you have an ol' lady?"

"Hadley!" I fussed.

"Nope." He shrugged. "Haven't found the one."

"What about you, Blaze?" she continued.

I was ready to pop a knot on her head when Blaze said, "Had one. Kevin's mother … she passed away a few years ago. Doubt I'll ever find anyone that could get to me like she did."

The table fell silent, and I was thankful that Hadley stopped talking and finished her breakfast. Once everyone was done eating, we got back on the road and headed for Casper. The closer we got, the more nervous I became. Meeting Clutch's brothers for the first time had me feeling anxious. From the stories he'd told, I already felt like I knew them. I knew they were good guys and I wish we were meeting under different circumstances. I couldn't imagine that they were happy about driving so far to rescue some chick and two kids who were running from some psycho killer. Unfortunately, I didn't have a choice. I'd have to suck it up and try to make the best of it.

When we finally made it to Casper, it was just after five, and we were all long past needing a break. With T-Bone following close behind, Blaze pulled into a busy truck stop parking lot. We'd barely had a chance to stretch our legs when two bikers pulled up next to us. As soon as they took off their helmets, I knew they were Maverick and Smokey. They were both exactly as Clutch had described them. Maverick was a pretty big guy with an athletic build, and he had short dark hair and these amazing green eyes. Smokey was a little taller and not as thick as Maverick, and his hair was tousled around his face, making it difficult to see his blue eyes. Like Maverick, he was attractive, but when he smiled, I could see why the ladies were so crazy about him.

Smokey walked over to me and said, "So you're the one that Clutch has been going on and on about."

"Yeah, I guess that'd be me, and you must be Smokey," I answered.

"The one and only. Nice to finally meet ya."

"You, too. Thanks for coming to get us like this. I really appreciate it."

"Don't mention it, doll. That's what we're here for." He looked over to Maverick and said, "I'm gonna take them inside and get them something to eat."

Maverick said, "Go ahead. I'll be there in a minute."

I tapped on the truck to get the kids' attention and motioned them to follow me and Smokey into the diner. The place was packed with truckers, but we still managed to find a table in the back. It wasn't long before Maverick walked in and joined us.

As soon as he sat down, he said, "So, you're Clutch's ol' lady, huh?"

"I guess you could say that." I smiled.

With a smirk, he replied, "Figured a girl like you would be smarter than that."

I shrugged and said, "I don't know about that. I figure *he's* the one who's not so smart, getting tangled up with me. I've got baggage for days."

Smokey looked at me and, with a seriousness in his voice, said, "We've all got baggage, doll. It's what you do with it that counts. From what Clutch has said, you've been doing just fine with yours."

"Yeah ... up until about thirty-six hours ago, I was doing alright. But I've been told that sometimes you have to go through hell before you can get to the good. I'm hoping the good will hurry up and get here."

"It will come. Don't you worry about that," Maverick told me. "But we need to get you home before Clutch has a complete come-apart. If you're up for it, we'll drive a couple more hours, and then find a place to stop for the night."

I nodded. "I'm good with that."

Hadley looked up from her menu and asked, "How far is it to Washington?"

"It's a pretty long haul, but we should be there sometime tomorrow," he answered.

"Are we really going to stay at your clubhouse?" she asked.

Maverick smiled and answered, "That's the plan. We're gonna keep an eye on you until Clutch gets things sorted in Memphis."

I'd been so worried about leaving Clutch, thinking something might happen to him that I hadn't taken the time to think about the other side of the coin. I had no idea what he and his brothers planned on doing to the man that Sam found in the alley or what they'd do to the men who had killed my parents. I didn't know much about the club. In fact, I didn't know anything about the club, except they all wore the same patch on their leather jackets. I didn't know their rules or how things really worked in or out of the clubhouse. I sure as hell didn't know how they handled psycho killers, but honestly, I didn't care; I knew in my heart that they'd do whatever it took to keep me and the kids safe, and that was the only thing that mattered.

Chapter 22
Clutch

"You got yourself a real stunner, brother," Smoke taunted.

Ignoring him, I asked, "Where are you?"

"We're at a hotel just outside of Billings. Just got Olivia and the kids settled in their room."

"Is she doing okay?"

He paused for a minute and then answered, "It's a lot, man. She and those kids have been through the ringer, but she's a tough one. She'll be alright. Don't worry. We've got it covered. What about you? What's going on there?"

"Rick made the call. He should be coming into Memphis by tomorrow afternoon."

"Any idea who this guy is?"

"That's the kicker. We've still got no fucking idea. Crow's been working on it, but this guy is playing it smart. He's using a burner phone, and he used an offshore bank account to wire the money into Rick's account. There's no way to trace this guy, but by this time tomorrow, it won't matter who the fuck he is. He's dead either way."

"I don't know, man. You need to be careful. Sounds like this guy knows what he's doing," Smoke warned.

"Been thinking the same thing. Hard to believe that Perry's son would know how to pull all this shit off."

"Maybe it was Hanson, or at least someone Hanson paid to handle it. He's got the means to do it," Smokey told me.

"Yeah, I know he's got the means, but why would he go to all this trouble over some fucking real estate? It doesn't add up."

"Got no idea, but you and I both know people do some crazy shit for money," Smoke replied. "I better get going. Need to catch some Z's, man. Got a long one tomorrow. I'll touch base when we make a stop."

"Sounds good. Watch after my girl," I ordered.

"You know I will," he snickered before he hung up the phone.

I was just about to leave the clubhouse when I checked the time. It was after ten, so I assumed that Olivia and the kids had already gone to bed. I still wanted her to know I was thinking about her, so I sent her a text.

Me:
Missing you.

To my surprise, seconds later she responded.

L. Wilder

Liv:

Bet I miss you more.

Me:

Why aren't you sleeping?

Liv:

Because you texted me lol

Me:

Wasn't expecting you to answer.

Liv:

Then why did you text me?

Me:

Are you giving me a hard time?

Liv:

Maybe…

Me:

Get some sleep.

Liv:

I will, but not yet. I can't sleep.
What are you doing right now?

Clutch

Me:

Just leaving the clubhouse.

Heading back to the apartment to catch some Z's.

Liv:

So you're thinking about me, huh?

Me:

Always.

Liv:

I've been thinking about you too.

I really miss having you around.

Me:

Miss having you around, too.

But I'll be there with you soon enough.

Liv:

You promise?

Me:

Nothing in this world could keep me away from you.

Liv:

I don't know what's going on back there.

I don't want to know … It scares me.

Just promise me that you will be careful.

I need you here.

Me:

Promise.

Liv:

I love you.

Me:

Love you too, Sunshine.

Now get some sleep.

I'll talk to you tomorrow, baby.

Liv:

Okay. I'll try.

But promise me you will too!

XOXO

I shoved my phone in my back pocket and headed for my bike. I'd been at the club all day talking things over with the brothers and I was ready to call it a night. I'd only been home a few minutes when I felt the silence of the room crushing down on me. The absence of the constant hum of Olivia and the kids talking and moving around next door made me miss them even more. When I couldn't stand it any longer, I grabbed the TV remote and spent the next hour flipping through the channels on the TV. I finally picked one of those kid shows that Hadley was always watching and lay down on the sofa.

I shoved one of the cushions under my head and tried to go to sleep, but every time I closed my eyes, I saw Olivia staring back at me. Fuck. She'd only been gone a day and I was pining over her like some lovesick pup. That woman had gotten under my skin in a way that no woman ever had. It made me think about what my grandmother had told me a few months back. I really didn't get it at the time, but I finally understood what she meant now. As always, my grandmother was right. Olivia captivated my every thought to the point that I felt like I couldn't breathe without her. I did *ache* for her. I didn't give a fuck who had to go to the dirt to protect her. A love like Olivia's was worth fighting for, and I planned to put up one hell of a fight. I loved her, and there was nothing I wouldn't do to keep her and those kids safe.

I had no idea what time I'd finally fallen asleep or how long I'd actually been asleep, but the irritating sounds of kids singing pulled me from my slumber. After turning off the TV, I checked the time. It was almost eight, so I got up. After a quick shower, I headed for the club.

Church was in a couple of hours and I needed to check in with Crow to see if he'd gone over everything that Big Mike sent. I also needed to see if he'd been able to break through the firewall on that offshore bank account so we'd have a better idea of who we were dealing with. I wanted to have all the information in Gus's hands before we met with the brothers. He wanted everything laid out so we'd all be fully prepared for the night that lay ahead.

When I got to the club, most of the guys were gathered in the kitchen having breakfast while they waited for Gus to call church. The smell of bacon made my stomach growl with hunger, but I didn't have time to grab breakfast. I needed to talk to Crow, and since he wasn't in the kitchen, I headed straight to his room. The door was open, so I knocked as I stepped inside. He was already at his computer working, and when he looked up, I said, "Were you able to come up with anything?"

"Been at it all night, man. Every time I get close, I hit another wall. But I did find something," he answered as he pushed the piles of papers to the side and started typing on his laptop.

I walked over and sat down next to him as he pulled something up on the screen. "Whatcha got?"

"I'm not sure if she knows it, but Olivia's father left his share of the company to her. That's almost seventy percent of the company, so she's the final authority. Everything big is on hold with the rest of the development until she comes back home and signs off on the papers. From what I can tell, Turner's assistant has been doing the best he can to keep the company running the way the old man wanted. His name is Evan Matheny, and he seems pretty loyal. Been with Turner from the beginning and has always done right by him. I've hacked into all his shit, but unfortunately he doesn't know who killed his boss. He's trying to find Olivia and doing everything he can to protect the company within the executive authorities Turned had in place for him as his right-hand man. But right now, his hands are tied."

"Why's that?"

"Since her father's company still technically owns the remaining lots, they can't be sold until Olivia gives the okay," he explained. "They're stuck."

"What about Perry? What happened to his shares when he committed suicide?"

"His shares went to his son." Crow paused for a minute, then said, "You said Olivia thought these guys were after the kids because they might have seen something the night her parents were killed, but what if that wasn't it? What if they were after *her* as well?"

"That would make more sense," I replied. "Besides, if the kids had seen something, they would've already told the police."

"Exactly. She's told you all the information she knows. So, I'm thinking Olivia has no idea that she owns the shares of the company and that these guys most likely aren't just hunting the kids; they're also gunnin' for her."

"Fuck," I growled.

"This information doesn't change anything, brother," Crow started. "We end this shit tonight. I put a tracker on Rick's phone, hoping to get a ping on the guy's location that he's working for. I'll get him. One way or another, Olivia and those kids will have their life back."

"You got that right. Have you told Gus about this?"

"Yeah. I talked to him just before you got here. He's planning to go over everything with the guys in church. I'll have the name of your guy before you leave tonight. You have my word on that."

"Thanks, man," I told him as I stood to leave. "I owe you one."

"Hold on. I've got something else you might wanna see," he told me as he started sifting through the stack of papers on his desk. "Gus asked me to look into your buddy Sam. He wanted to see if there was something we might be able to do to help him out."

"And?"

"Did you know he was in the service?"

"Yeah, he mentioned something about it to Olivia a few months back. Said he was in the Navy or something."

Crow handed me a picture of a man in a full Navy service uniform with a variety of ribbons stretching across his left breast pocket and said, "That's Samuel Bennet. He was in the service for over twenty years until he was wounded in the USS Cole bombing. Seventeen sailors were killed and over thirty-nine were injured. Turns out, Sam was wounded while he was rescuing members of his crew. Even after he was hurt, he kept at it. Ended up being awarded a Bronze Star for saving six of his men from the fire."

I looked at the picture again as I asked, "This is our Sam?"

"The one and only."

"And now he's out choosing to live on the streets. That's fucked up, man."

He nodded in agreement as he said, "Yeah it is, but his life on the streets is done whether he likes it or not. Gus is going to make sure of it."

"Olivia will be relieved to hear that. Thanks for telling me," I told him as I headed for the door. Just before I left, I turned to him and said, "Funny how quickly things can change. Sam deserves a better life. I really hope he gets it."

Shortly after I finished up with Crow, the brothers met for church. Gus went over everything Crow had uncovered and we strategized our plans for tonight. Gus told us in church he'd talked to Cotton and assured him that there was no need to send any brothers from back home, because whoever was fucking with Olivia and the kids would be dead before they'd even have the time to get here. It felt good, knowing these brothers had my back. It didn't matter that they were our charter club; we were *all* Satan's Fury.

After we were done, Gus and I followed Bic and Crow to the warehouse. It was time for Rick to make another call to the fuckhead he was working for. Bic unlocked the door and we stepped inside. The small room reminded me of a jail cell. There was a cot in one corner and a sink and urinal in the other, and it reeked of piss and body odor. Rick was sitting at the end of the cot in his shirt soaked through with blood. His hair was greasy with sweat and grime, and he could barely keep his eyes open. Gus walked over to the sink and filled a glass with water, then poured it over Rick's head.

Rick sputtered and coughed as he pulled himself from his stupor, and when he looked like he actually knew we were standing there, Gus told him, "It's time to make another call."

"I think I'm dying," Rick muttered.

"You're not dying, asshole, but you will be if you fuck this up," Bic growled.

Gus stepped closer as he handed Rick his cell phone and said, "Make the call. Our man is tracking the call, so keep him on the line as long as you can. Do exactly what we've told you and I'll see about getting those wounds looked at."

"Okay," Rick mumbled as he took the phone in his hand.

"Fuck it up and I'll end you," Bic warned.

Rick dialed the number and waited for it to start ringing. He cleared his throat and then, several seconds later, he said, "Hey, man. What's your status?" He paused for a moment and then said, "Yeah. It's cool. I just checked. She's at the diner and the kids are upstairs in the apartment. They should all be home by the time you arrive." He nodded silently before saying, "Yeah, got it. It'll be a few hours before you get here, so I'll keep an eye on 'em and let you know if they make a move." He paused, trying to buy Crow a little more time, and then said, "Okay. Where? ... Fine. I was just wondering how long it will take you to get to her place. I doubt they'll go anywhere, but I will let you know if they do. Just give me a call when you get close and I'll let you know where they are." After another brief pause, he ended the call and handed the phone to Gus.

The second Crow gave me the nod that he'd gotten the information he needed, I asked Rick, "Where is he?"

"He's just leaving his house. He got a direct flight to Memphis and should be here by 7:00 pm. He said he's gotta make a stop somewhere and then he's heading straight to the apartment."

"What kind of stop?"

"He didn't say. I tried asking him, but he just said he had to make a stop," Rick repeated.

Gus looked over at Rick. "Hold tight. I'll get Mack in here to stitch you up."

"I'd appreciate it," Rick told him. There was hope in his voice as he asked, "Are you going to let me out of here?"

"That depends on you, Rick," Gus told him. "You do what we tell ya, and you'll be free to go when this is over. If not, then Bic gets to have a little fun with you."

As promised, Gus sent Mack in to tend to Rick's wounds while Crow worked his magic on finding our guy's exact location. Murph and I headed to the back to help Bic inspect all the artillery. Once all the weapons and ammo were checked, we loaded everything into the SUV. We were set to go. I had no idea how the night would play out, but I knew I had my brothers behind me and Olivia waiting for me back at home—and that's all I really needed to know.

Chapter 23
Olivia

I'd gone over everything Clutch had told me about
his brothers and the club a hundred times in my head,
but as soon as I walked through the front door, my mind
went blank from sensory overload. I was completely
overwhelmed and couldn't think straight. Before
Maverick went to check in with his ol' lady, he gave me
a quick tour of the clubhouse. Nothing was like I'd
imagined it would be. The place was huge with a bar
attached to the side and a maze of hallways that lead to
different rooms throughout the clubhouse. There was no
way I'd find my way around the place without help, but
luckily I didn't have to look far; there were plenty of
people around to ask. I tried to remember everyone's
names as they greeted me, but there were just so many
of them. While the men all had the look of badass
bikers, they were all very kind and welcomed me and
the kids like they'd known us forever.

When Guardrail showed us where we would be
staying, I was surprised to find that they had prepared
two adjoining rooms for us. Charlie would have a place
of his own, but he'd still be close enough for me to keep

an eye on him. After an hour or so, we were all unpacked and settling in. Even though it was still pretty early, the kids were exhausted, so they stretched out on my bed and turned on the TV. They'd just found a movie to watch when Cassidy stopped in to check on us. She chatted with the kids a minute, introducing herself as she unloaded a huge bag ironically full of all their favorite snacks and drinks. She even had a four-pack of my beloved banana split yogurt and an assortment of our favorite must-have fruits. Cassidy handed Charlie a programmed burner phone, explaining the contacts as she loaded the mini-fridge. It took some convincing, but she was persistent, and after assuring me the kids would be fine and could call if they needed anything, she managed to get me to come have a drink and visit with the ol' ladies.

We'd been sitting at the bar talking for almost an hour while I was listening to Allison explain how she met Guardrail. I overheard Wren turn to Henley and say, "She's really tall."

"Well, Clutch is, like, nine feet tall. A guy like him needs a tall girl at his side," Henley chuckled.

"True. I guess it will help balance him out," Wren said and laughed. "Have you looked at her hair? I just love it. It's the perfect mix of red and brown. It really brings out her eyes."

"Yeah, her eyes are so mystical, they look magical. Every time I look at them, they are a different color. Once minute they look green, and then all of a sudden they look brown." During the drive here, I'd gotten a chance to talk to Maverick, and he'd tried to warn me that his ol' lady Henley was a bit of a nut. He was right, but I liked her. Even though she was gorgeous, she had a smile that set me at ease.

Wren smiled and said, "I wish I had her skin. It's flawless. Since the pregnancy, mine has been a hot mess."

Wren was a little older than Henley, but she was also beautiful. When she mentioned my complexion, I had no idea what she was talking about. Even with her pregnancy, her skin looked absolutely perfect and seemed to glow. Glancing at Alison, who'd gone silent listening to Wren and Henley, I gave her a wink as I took a drink of my water, audibly cleared my throat, and then pointed to myself as I teasingly asked, "You do know I'm sitting right here?"

Cassidy laughed and said, "Don't mind them. All those pregnancy hormones have fried their brains."

There was something different about Cassidy. From the start, I could see that there was a curiosity behind her eyes when she talked to me. I assumed it had something to do with being the president's ol' lady, so I did my best to ignore it. I looked over to Henley and noticed that she was six or seven months along while Wren was barely showing, so I asked, "When are you both due?"

Henley answered, "In an eternity from now."

Cassidy shook her head. "Not an eternity. You just

have two and a half more months to go."

"That's an eternity! This little twerp keeps kicking my bladder. I'm in the bathroom every five minutes," Henley groaned. "But it will be worth it in a few months to have a little Maverick running around."

"Are you sure you can't do something about that?" Cassidy teased. "One Maverick is enough."

"I'm so gonna tell him you said that," Henley growled, and then out of nowhere, she suddenly turned her attention towards me. Her lips curled into a mischievous grin as she said, "So you've heard our stories from Clutch. You know I'm with Maverick, and Guardrail is with Allie. You know Wren is Stitch's ol' lady and Cassidy is with Cotton." She waved her hand in the air as she continued, "Their stories are old and boring. We've heard them a hundred times. Now we want to know all about you and Clutch. How'd you two hook up?"

I shrugged, suddenly feeling shy with all four sets of their eyes on me. "I don't know. We met at the diner where I worked. Other than that, I guess there's not much to say."

"Somehow, I doubt that," Henley said. "With Clutch, there is always something to say."

I glanced at Henley, giving her a small smile. Stalling for a minute, I sat circling the top of my water bottle with a fingertip, trying to find the words. I didn't know how to explain to these women how deeply I felt for Clutch, how powerful our love felt to me. I didn't know these women, and they were all his people ... his family.

"Well, to tell the truth ... we had a bit of a rocky start," I confessed. "I was just trying to keep my head above water when he showed up. Starting something with anyone was the last thing on my mind at the time. At first, I was kind of ticked at him for being so good-looking ... No, I take that back. I was really, really mad at him for being so damn good-looking," I said with a smile. "From the second I met him, he completely unhinged me. Just his presence alone awakened something uncontrollable inside me. I felt a pull towards him like I'd never felt before. He was so hot, I couldn't keep my eyes or my mind off of him, and I hated feeling so consumed."

Their eyes were all on me.

So I continued. "It didn't help that he was there every time I turned around. He was a distraction that I felt for certain I didn't need in my life. I was sure he was nothing but hot as hell trouble, and I knew we were a whole different level of trouble *he* definitely didn't need. But I was selfish, and he kept pulling me in with that sexy little smile and all the sweet things he'd do. He seemed to understand what we were going through without me even telling him—better than *we* even understood, truthfully. We all became attached to him pretty fast. He ... made us feel like ourselves. His presence awakened what we didn't even realize we'd lost after my parents' deaths. He pulled us into the present. I couldn't help myself. He was just too easy to fall in love with. It was like he was my knight in shining armor, but instead of riding on a big white horse, he was riding a big black *iron* horse."

Cassidy gave me a strange look, then said, "You really love him, don't you?"

"Yeah. I really do."

"I'm glad to hear that. Clutch is a really good guy. I'm glad he found you."

"I'm glad he did, too. And he couldn't have come at a better time. We needed him in more ways than I could ever imagine."

"Maverick said you've been taking care of your brother and sister after your parents were killed. That had to be hard," Henley told me.

I shrugged and said, "They're my family. There's nothing in the world I wouldn't do for them. And honestly, I wouldn't have been able to make it through this whole thing without them. Maybe this will all be over soon and we can get back to a normal life."

"You will. It will just take some time," Wren assured me.

Just thinking about it made me miss Clutch even more, so I decided to change the subject. "Do you know what you're having? Have you thought of any names?"

"No names yet, but we found out the other day that we're having a little girl," Wren answered, beaming with pride.

"A little girl! That's awesome, Wren. Why didn't

you tell us sooner?" Henley asked.

"We've just had so much going on, and Stitch ..." she started, but stopped.

"What about Stitch?" Henley pushed.

"He's acting a little weird ever since we got the news from the doctor. I think he might be a little disappointed," Wren explained. As she was talking, Stitch came up behind her.

Before I had a chance to warn her that he was there, Stitch asked, "Disappointed about what?"

Her eyes widened with surprise when she heard his voice, and her face flushed red as she turned around to face him. Her eyes dropped to her hands as she answered, "I was just telling them that I thought you might be a little disappointed that we weren't having a boy."

His eyebrows furrowed, but not in anger. He seemed completely surprised by her response. The strong man covered in tattoos and a full beard turned completely soft as he placed his hand on her belly and said, "Darlin', the minute I saw this little girl on that computer screen, I knew she'd already wrapped me around her little finger ... just like her momma. I'm just worried ... not sure I'll ever be able to tell her no, so you'll have to be the one who does that."

She looked up at him and smiled. "I think we'll manage." She wrapped her hands around his neck. "I love you, Griffin, and you're going to be an amazing father to our little girl just like you already are with

Wyatt."

He kissed her lightly on the lips and said, "It's getting late. We need to get Wyatt home so he can get some sleep."

He took her hand in his, then helped her step down from her stool. She turned to me and said, "It was really nice to meet you, Olivia. I think you're going to make a great addition to the crew."

"Thanks, Wren. It was great to meet you, too," I told her. As soon as they were gone, I stood up. "I guess I better get going. It's been a really long day and I need to check on the kids."

"Okay. Try to get some rest," Cassidy urged me. "There's plenty of food in the fridge if the kids get hungry. Just help yourself."

"Thanks. I'll let them know," I told her as I headed for my room.

When I walked in, Hadley was already sound asleep while Charlie was close behind her. He rubbed his eyes and yawned before he said, "How was it?"

"It was fun. They are all really nice," I answered as I sat down at the foot of the bed.

"Have you heard from Clutch?"

I looked down at my watch and my stomach sank when I realized I hadn't heard from him in hours. I feigned a smile and said, "He'll call in a little while."

"You're worried. I can tell."

"Maybe a little, but I'm sure everything will be okay."

"What do you think they are going to do?" Charlie asked with concern.

"Do about what?"

"You know, with the guys that are after us. What do you think they'll do to them?"

"I don't know, Charlie. I just know that Clutch is going to do whatever it takes to make sure we're safe. That's all that really matters."

"I really like him, Livie. He's a good guy."

"Yeah, I think so, too."

Charlie gave me a quick hug before he went next door to his room. I crawled into bed next to Hadley and tried to go to sleep, but it was pointless. There was no way I was going to be able to get any rest until I knew Clutch was okay. I reached for my phone and laid it next to my head, praying that it would ring, but it never did.

Chapter 24
Clutch

Cyrus loaded Rick into the back of the SUV, and I was just about to join him when Gus called out to me. He was talking on the phone and motioned me over to him as he said, "Hold on. The tracker worked. Crow got the son-of-a-bitch." After several minutes, Gus hung up the phone and said, "It's Perry's son, Daniel."

"Damn it. I knew it was that motherfucker," I growled.

"Once Crow got the address and tracked it to Daniel, he was able to hack into all of his information and link it to the offshore bank accounts that paid Rick. He also found out that he'd paid a guy named Jonathan Tate a hundred and fifty grand the night Olivia's parents were killed. Must have been too chicken-shit to commit murder on his own. He just paid the guy another hundred grand yesterday along with a plane ticket to Memphis. Tate isn't affiliated with any organization, so we won't have to worry about any blowback from him. According to Crow's intel, the two met at a shooting range six months ago. Tate's an alcoholic hermit doomsday prepper," Gus explained, shaking his head.

"Looks like he won't be alone tonight."

"Depending on what they were able to bring on the plane, they might be stopping somewhere to get more guns and ammo before they get here," Bic added.

"I'll have Crow keep an eye on it," Gus told him. "But for now, it's time for us to roll out."

We all piled into the SUV and headed towards Olivia's apartment. Once we got there, Cyrus pulled Rick out of the truck and had him make one final call to Daniel. As soon as he answered, Rick told him, "They're still home. I've been watching the place all night. I think they're in their rooms, from what I can tell. They turned the living room lights off about thirty minutes ago. Yeah, just like I told you. It's the apartment above Daisy's Diner on Front Street. The first one at the top of the stairs." He paused and then said, "Yeah, they're all there and it's just them. Been up there for a while now." Before he hung up, Rick asked, "Hey, man. When will I get the other half of my money?" Unfortunately for him, the line went dead before he got his answer. Rick grumbled, "Lying bastard. Bet ten to one he doesn't pay me another dime."

"Yeah, it's not looking good for you there, buddy," Cyrus chuckled as he yanked him back over to the SUV and locked him inside.

Within the hour, we were in Olivia's apartment. It felt strange being there. The place didn't look the same without her in it. We got to our posts. With Crow monitoring the surveillance feeds from the cameras they'd installed the day before, we'd have no problem knowing exactly when Daniel entered the building. Lowball and a couple of prospects were holed up outside in the hallway and Gus and Murph were in the kitchen while Cyrus and I waited by the front door with our weapons drawn. Since the club owned the diner and the apartments upstairs, we didn't have to be concerned about anyone reporting gunfire. We had everything covered, and now all we had to do was wait.

Luckily we didn't have to wait long before Crow's voice came through our two-way radio, letting us know that Daniel had just parked his rental car in the back lot. With Tate in the lead, they started up the back steps. Crow continued to inform us of every move they made until they reached Olivia's front door. The tension in the room crackled around me as I watched the door handle turn. Knowing they were just on the other side, I had to fight the urge to yank the door open and just end them both right then and there. I took a deep breath and held myself together.

Eventually, the door crept open, and my heart began to pound against my chest as Tate slowly slipped inside. He was a big guy, and he reeked of cigarettes and cheap liquor. I was about to come unglued with impatience when seconds later, Daniel followed in behind him. He was tall and lanky, and the idiot thought he was being clever by wearing all black, right down to the gloves and ski mask, like some burglar he'd seen on

TV. Just seeing him made me want to punch him in the face.

The door clicked shut, and just as Tate took a step forward, he spotted the reflection of one of the guys in the kitchen.

"Fuck!" he shouted as he aimed his gun at Murph, but before he had a chance to shoot, Gus nailed him right between the eyes. Blood gushed from his wound as his lifeless body dropped to the ground.

Daniel froze. I stepped up behind him and said, "Surprise, surprise, motherfucker. Don't you know better than to mess with a biker's ol' lady?"

I didn't give him a chance to answer. Instead, I took the butt of the gun and slammed it against the back of his head, making him drop to the ground like a two-ton lead weight. By the time he started to wake up, Cyrus had already bound and gagged him to a chair. We didn't have to worry about anyone hearing him scream, but Cyrus got a kick out of shoving a dirty sock down the fucker's throat, hoping that he'd gag on it as he came to. And sure enough, the minute he opened his eyes, he started coughing and gagging like the pathetic little bitch that he was.

Daniel's eyes roamed across the room. Panic washed over his face when he noticed all of my brothers standing around him. Gus walked over to him and grabbed a fistful of his hair as he said, "Not gonna sugarcoat this, Daniel. As of tonight, you're done. We're going to dump your sorry piece of shit ass into the fucking river, but before we do that, my man Clutch has a few questions for you."

He released him just as Bic started towards him with one of his long, sharp blades. Daniel's face twisted with fear as Bic took the knife and pressed it against his chest, applying enough pressure to slice through the cotton fabric of his black t-shirt and gouge into the first few layers of his skin. Blood began to seep down Daniel's chest as Bic knelt down in front of him. While twisting the knife still embedded in Daniel's chest, he said, "My brother has a few questions for you. You answer him, and this will go a whole lot easier for you."

Daniel nodded frantically as Bic pulled the sock from his mouth. I didn't move from my spot as I asked, "Who else was involved?"

"Involved in what?" he spat.

Bic took his knife and quickly jabbed it deep into Daniel's thigh, leaving it there as a reminder that there was more to come. His body instantly curled against his restraints as he groaned out in pain. As he lowered his head and pissed himself, his body began to tremble uncontrollably. I could see he'd resigned himself to the reality of his imminent demise. I stepped over to him and asked again, "Who else was involved?"

With a whimper, he answered, "Me. It was just me."

"Hanson had nothing to do with it?" I asked.

"No," he groaned. "He'd never have gone along with it. It was just me. I had to do it to get the deal done."

"And your old man?"

He paused for a minute, then snarled, "What about him?"

I grabbed him by the throat, squeezing tightly against his windpipe as I growled, "Was he involved?"

The veins in his face began to rise to the surface as I kept my hold on his throat, and when I finally released him, he coughed and groaned, "No." Once he'd caught his breath, he continued, "When he wouldn't go along with my plan, I blackmailed him. Told him I'd make the police think he'd done it."

"Is that why he killed himself?" I asked out of curiosity.

His face hardened as he said, "When he continued to refuse me, I killed him and made it look like a suicide."

The guy was off his fucking rocker. His lust for money would be his demise, and I couldn't think of a person who deserved it more. Once he'd confirmed that there was no one else involved, it was done. Nothing else mattered. I gave the nod to Gus, and within a couple of hours, I was on my bike headed home to Olivia and the kids.

Chapter 25

Olivia

It was still dark when I stepped outside. I'd been trying for hours, but I just couldn't sleep, so I thought some fresh air might help. A cool breeze whipped around me as I walked over to one of the picnic tables and sat down. It was so quiet, nothing like it usually was. All the constant talking and scuffling around was gone, and it was just me and a hint of the sun rising over the mountaintops. I took a deep breath, trying to calm my rattled nerves, but it was no use. I'd been up all night waiting for Clutch to call, but I never heard from him. It wasn't like him not to check in, so I couldn't help but think something was wrong. When I was just about to have a complete come-apart, Smokey came around the corner smiling like the cat that ate the canary. He was rocking some serious bed head and his clothes were disheveled like he'd been up to something.

"Hey there, doll. What are you doing out here all alone?" he asked. He looked like he might still be a little drunk from the night before as he swayed over to me.

"Couldn't sleep," I answered.

"You got something on your mind?" He sat down next to me and lit a cigarette as he waited for me to answer.

"Just worried. Clutch didn't call last night," I told him as I tried to hold back my tears.

"You've got nothing to worry about, sweetheart. Clutch is probably halfway home by now."

"You really think so?"

"Yeah. He probably thought he was doing you a favor by not calling so late, like he thought he'd wake you or the kids or something. You know, us guys can be kinda stupid about stuff like that."

"Hmmm … I'm not even going to comment on that one," I laughed.

"See? You're a smart ol' lady. You know when not to say stuff or do stuff. Us guys … we're always getting ourselves into trouble. Well, at least I am." He grinned.

I pointed at his clothes and teased, "Looks like you might have gotten yourself into some trouble last night."

"You have no idea."

"A girlfriend?"

"Nah, haven't found the one yet. I thought I had found her …" he started, but stopped and flicked his cigarette to the ground. He stood up and said, "But what the hell do I know? Clutch thought he'd found the one in Cass, but he was obviously wrong about that. He's head over heels for you. She's just a distant memory."

"Cass? You mean Cassidy?"

His eyes widened as he realized what he'd just said.

He quickly tried to fix it by adding, "It was nothing, doll. A lifetime ago."

"Hold up ... Clutch and Cass were together?"

"No. It wasn't like that. He just ... you know ... had a thing for her or something," Smokey stammered.

I felt like the wind had been knocked out of me. I ran my hand through my hair as I tried to swallow my tears and said, "He had a thing for her? That's even worse." I really liked Cassidy, but the thought of Clutch having feelings for her made me second-guess everything.

"You're getting me all wrong here, doll. You've got nothing to worry about."

"I'm not so sure about that. Clutch never said anything to me about his feelings for her," I told him with concern.

He placed his hand on my arm as he said, "No reason to. He loves you. I can hear it in his voice when he talks about you. He's never been like this with a woman, Olivia. He's nuts over you, and the past is just that: the past."

"If you say so," I mumbled.

"I do say so, and if you think about it, you'll know I'm right." He brushed his hair out of his eyes as he stood up and said, "Come on. Let's go inside. We both could use a few hours of sleep before we have to face this crazy bunch."

"Okay." I followed him inside, and as he turned to leave, I said, "You're a good one, Smokey. The right one will come along soon."

"We'll see about that." He smiled. "Get some rest. He'll be home before you know it."

I headed back to my room and got back in bed, trying my best to get some sleep. Unfortunately, I just ended up staring at the ceiling hour after hour. I couldn't stop thinking about what Smokey had said about Clutch's feelings for Cassidy. It was crazy for me to think that he hadn't been in love before, but I couldn't help but wonder why he hadn't even mentioned it. He'd told me so much about the club and his brothers, but her name never came up. I found myself worrying that there might be a reason that he kept it from me. She was beautiful and kind, and I could see why he might fall for her.

But maybe Smokey was right. Maybe there really wasn't anything for me to worry about. I'd seen the way that she looked at Cotton with absolute love in her eyes. I couldn't imagine her with anyone else. They seemed totally in love with each other. I went over it again and again in my head and tried to make myself believe the past didn't matter. I was still lost in my thoughts when I heard my phone ding with a message. I quickly grabbed it off the nightstand and all my thoughts of Cass immediately vanished when I saw that it was Clutch.

Clutch:

Morning, Sunshine. I'm headed that way. It's done.

Me:

It's really over?

Clutch:

It's really over.

Me:

Why didn't you call last night?
You had me scared to death.

Clutch:

I sent you a message last night. Check your phone.

Sure enough, when I scrolled up, three messages from him popped up on my screen. The stupid burner had been screwing up since Clutch had given it to me before we left for the clubhouse, and I decided right then I was getting a *real* phone as soon as possible.

Mc:

I hate this phone. They just came through.

Clutch:

Sorry I had you worried.
I will call tonight when I stop for the night.

Me:

Okay. Can't wait to see you. Be careful.

Clutch

Clutch:
Always.

Thankfully it was Sunday, so most of the guys had gone home to spend time with their families. With only a few quick breaks to grab something to eat in the kitchen, the kids and I spent most of the afternoon watching movies in my room. Just as we were getting ready for bed, Clutch called to let me know that he would be home late the following afternoon. Knowing that he was really okay, I was finally able to get a good night's sleep. The following morning, I slept in late, and by the time I had gotten up and had my shower, the kids were nowhere to be found. Worried that they might be into something, I tried to find them. I still didn't know my way around very well so I got completely turned around and ended up running into Cotton as he was coming out of his office.

He smiled and asked, "Hey, Olivia. Is everything alright?"

"Yes. Everything is good." I laughed anxiously. The man seemed perfectly nice with his salt and pepper hair and kind eyes, but he was the president of Clutch's club. The last thing I wanted to do was say the wrong thing. My mind went completely blank as I stood there just staring at him, but I finally managed to blurt out, "I was just looking for the kids and got a little lost."

His lips curled into a smile as he said, "I bet they are in the game room. It's just down the hall on your left."

"I'll go check. Thanks." Still feeling nervous, I smiled and walked down the hall.

Just as I was about to turn into the game room, Cotton yelled, "Olivia?"

I turned to face him. "Yes?"

"Your other left." He laughed as he pointed to the room across the hall from where I was standing.

I threw my hands up in the air as I shook my head and shouted, "Thank you!"

I felt like a complete idiot as I turned around and entered the correct room. Thankfully, Hadley and Charlie were there playing some crazy game on the club's gaming system. I sat down on the sofa and watched as they played basketball, some crazy war game, and by the time they started their third game, I'd just about had enough. The blaring noise from the television and their excited screams were giving me a headache, and I thought I would just about lose my mind until Cassidy came to rescue me.

My mind went straight back to my conversation with Smokey as she stood in the doorway and asked, "We're making up some hamburgers for the guys to grill out. Would you and the kids like to join us?"

In a different circumstance, I might have hesitated, but the thought of staying in that room for one more second had me jumping up from the sofa. "Sure! That would be great. Is there anything I can do to help?"

"Absolutely," she answered. "Come with me to the

kitchen and we'll get things started."

In just a couple of hours, we had everything set to go: chips and dip, beans, potato salad, and tons of desserts. Several of the guys were gathered around the grill cooking the burgers while Henley and I helped Cassidy set everything out on the picnic tables. When I looked around, it wasn't difficult to see why Clutch loved the club like he did. They were all like one big family, and I felt blessed just to be there with them. The more I was around Cassidy, the more I decided that I truly liked her. She had been so sweet to make me feel a part of the group, and it meant the world to me.

I was so busy helping her get dinner ready that I hadn't realized Clutch had walked up. Apparently he was just standing there watching me, and I would have never known if I hadn't seen Cassidy smiling at someone behind me. Just as I was turning around, he reached for me, lifting me in his arms, and he pulled me close as he kissed me. As the heat of his kiss traveled through my veins, I melted into his arms, completely forgetting that we were surrounded by his brothers and their families.

He slowly lowered me to the ground as he released me from our embrace and whispered, "Don't move."

I watched with wonder as he walked over to his brothers and greeted each of them with a heartfelt hug. From the smiles on their faces, it was obvious that they were all pleased to see that their brother had come back home. After only talking to them for a few minutes, he returned to me, and as he reached for my hand, he smiled and said, "Gonna need some time alone with you. Like, now."

"I could go for that." I laughed as I followed him into the clubhouse.

He led me to his room and, once we were inside, he kissed me once more. "Been on the road for twelve hours with one thing on my mind."

"And what would that be?" I smiled.

"You," he answered. "Now, I'm going to take a quick shower, and when I get out, I'm going to take you over to that bed and make love to you until I pass out from exhaustion."

"Okay," I giggled.

When he stepped into the bathroom, he shouted, "On second thought, I've been on a bike all day. It's about time for you to do some of the riding."

"Just hurry up, Shaggy," I teased as he turned on the shower. "It's not nice to keep a girl waiting ... especially when she's missed you as much as I have."

"So my girl has been missing me, huh?"

"Maybe ... just a little."

"Hmmm ... I must be slipping on my game then," he chuckled.

"Clutch?" I called out to him.

"Yeah?"

"I love you."

Chapter 26
Clutch

When I stepped back into the room, she was waiting for me wearing only a black lace bra and sexy-as-hell black low-cut panties. I took one look at her and everything that had happened over the past few days became a distant memory.

She walked over to me, and her arms, soft and smooth, wrapped around my neck. I covered her mouth with mine, and in that moment, it felt like my entire world was centered right there in her arms. I wanted to be gentle, to savor every moment we had, but I didn't have the strength to restrain myself. I was completely lost in her—the scent of her hair, the feel of her heart beating against her chest, the taste of her skin. I slipped the straps of her bra from her shoulders, letting them slide ever so slowly down her body as I continued to claim her mouth. She shivered when I moved from her lips to her breast, then gasped as I skimmed my teeth over her nipple and drew it deep into my mouth. Her lust-filled eyes met mine as I slowly lowered my hands down to her perfect hips and removed her lace panties, tossing them to the floor.

I led her over to the bed, releasing her only for a moment while I dropped my towel to the floor and rolled on a condom. I lay down as she climbed onto me, positioning her knees at my side and straddling me. She hovered over me, hesitating for only a moment, before she opened for me to slip deep inside her. Her eyes closed tightly as she gasped with pleasure. Then, her face softened as she placed the palms of her hands against my chest and said, "I missed you."

"I missed you, too. More than you could possibly know."

The world around us melted away. It was just the two of us. Nothing else mattered. I knew I'd found the love that I'd been searching for and that I'd spend the rest of my life giving her all I had to give. Her thighs tightened as she began to rock against me in a slow and steady pace. I heard my name slip from her lips, making my heart pound as I looked up at her. Damn, she was so fucking beautiful, like my very own angel sent from above.

Her muscles quivered as she continued to writhe in slow, silky movements. We were both coming close to the edge. She cried out in pleasure as her head fell back and her body jolted above me, her nails biting into my shoulders as her pace quickened. I let my hand slip down between her thighs, my thumb sliding over her clit as her body bucked against my touch. Her moans filled the room as I brought her closer to her release. I loved to watch her mouth form a perfect O as her body clenched in ecstasy with each rock of her hips. It seemed like ages since I'd been inside of her, and I was fighting with everything I had not to come right then and there. Panting and breathless, she clamped down around my cock, making me even harder, and said in barely a whisper, "So close."

"Let it go, baby. I'm right here with you," I told her as I placed my hands on her hips, guiding her into a demanding pace. Her body began to tremble with her impending orgasm, and when it finally broke, I couldn't hold back any longer.

"Fuck!" I roared as my hands went to her hips, holding her firmly in place as I came.

She collapsed on top of me with her head resting on my shoulder as she whispered, "I really did miss you."

"I missed you, too," I told her as I ran my fingers through her hair.

She slowly eased off of me and curled into my side as she said, "Smokey told me about you and Cass."

"Yeah?"

"He said I didn't have anything to worry about," she continued. "Was he right?"

I turned to face her. Seeing the worried look in her eyes gutted me. With the back of my fingertips, I stroked her cheek. "There was a time I thought I loved her ... but I was wrong. I had no idea what love really was until I met you. Nothing could compare to the way I feel about you. You're it for me, Liv."

"You're it for me, too." She smiled, then paused for a minute before saying, "I can't believe it's all really over. Can we finally move on and stop worrying that someone is after us?"

"Yes, but there are some things you need to know..." I started.

She raised her head and looked at me as she said, "No ... I don't want to know anything about it."

"This is something you have to know, Liv. It's about your father's company."

With a curious look, she asked, "What about his company?"

"He left his shares of the company to you. You are now the major shareholder to one of the largest real estate companies in Massachusetts."

She stared at me for a minute as she processed what I'd just told her. Then she said, "What if I don't want it?"

"Why wouldn't you want it?"

"My father loved selling real estate. It was his passion, but I have no idea how to run a company like that. I would ruin what he worked so hard to build."

"I doubt that."

"I don't want to take that chance," she said adamantly.

"What about your father's assistant Evan? Maybe he could help," I suggested. "From what we were able to find out, he seems loyal to your father."

"That's a great idea. I'll just give it to him," she

said, sounding relieved.

"Liv ... your father's company is worth millions. You don't just *give* it to him," I laughed.

"You know what I mean. He knows how things work, and he can keep things running the way they are supposed to."

"You've got time. You'll get it sorted."

"I don't know what the man was thinking."

"Your dad wouldn't have left it to you if he didn't think you could handle it, and I happen to think he's right."

She started trailing the tip of her finger over the lines of my tattoo as she lost herself in her thoughts. Several minutes passed before she looked back up at me and said, "What happens now?"

"With what?"

"With us ... the kids. I don't know. All of it. We'll need to figure things out."

"Nothing to figure out, Liv. Tomorrow, we'll get you and the kids settled at my house. By the end of the week, we'll get them enrolled in school."

"So that's it, huh?" she asked.

"Yeah ... pretty much. You're mine, Liv, and now that I have you and those kids here with me, there's no way I'm going to let you go."

"Just so you know, I wasn't planning on going anywhere. I like it here." She smiled. "And while I am thinking about it, aren't your brothers going to wonder where you are?"

"Darlin', there's not a man out there who doesn't know where I am and what I'm doing," I teased.

A light blush crossed her beautiful face as she said, "Seriously? You had to say that?"

"It's the truth," I laughed. "But, you're right. We should grab a bite to eat, and check on the kids."

We both lay there silently for a few minutes until she finally said, "Okay ... I am going to pry myself out of this bed and take a quick shower." She eased herself up. As she headed into the bathroom, she added, "I'm glad you're home."

As soon as I heard the water turn on, I pulled myself out of bed and joined her where I couldn't help but have one more go with her before we headed outside.

It had been months since I'd seen my brothers, but when we started talking, it was like I'd never been gone. Smokey and I were talking when Cotton walked over and said, "I need a minute." I nodded and followed him into the bar. As soon as we were seated, he said, "Looks like you got your shit sorted."

"I did," I agreed. "Appreciate you giving me the time."

"You did good, mapping out the pipeline. Everything will be set to go in the next couple of weeks. You gonna be ready for that?"

"Absolutely," I answered.

"Good to have you back, brother," he told me as he stood to leave. "You need help getting Olivia and the kids settled, just let us know."

"Will do."

I reached into the cooler for a beer and followed him back outside. Cassidy was standing by one of the picnic tables talking to Olivia, and when she saw me coming towards them, a warm smile spread across her face. Only a few months ago, I thought I'd never want to see her again, thought it would be too hard, but seeing her there talking with Olivia and being the loving person I'd always known her to be made me realize just how much I'd missed her. It was nothing like the way I had missed Olivia. The feeling I had for her was much different. She was a good friend, and I'd let my misguided feelings for her almost ruin everything. But time had a way of putting things in perspective, and I knew if anyone would understand why I had to walk away, it would be her.

I walked over to her and gave her a quick hug as I said, "Good to see you, Cass."

"Glad you finally made your way back. We've missed you around here."

"It's good to be back."

Cassidy looked over at Olivia and smiled as she said, "You got a good one here. She fits right in."

I wrapped my arm around Olivia's waist as I pulled her to my side and said, "Yeah, I think she's a keeper."

"Definitely a keeper." Cass smiled.

Olivia cleared her throat and smiled as she said, "Umm, you do know I am standing right here. Right?"

I looked down at her and, just before I kissed her, I said, "Yeah, I think you'll fit in just fine."

Epilogue

Three years later.

I'd heard that time had a way of healing all wounds, but for a long time, I had my doubts. I never thought I'd be able to find true happiness after I lost my parents and the life I'd created back in Boston, but I did. I was truly happy, and the kids were, too. Clutch and I had built a life together, a good life, and each day seemed to get better and better.

"Every one of these cereals has marshmallows in it," I told Clutch as he walked into the kitchen.

"And?" he smiled.

"And ... they all have marshmallows, Clutch," I scolded.

"Not sure I get your point." He shrugged his shoulders and laughed as he said, "Besides, the kids like them."

"The kids like ice cream, too, but that doesn't mean they should eat it for breakfast."

"Ice cream has dairy in it. It's not so bad." When I just stood there staring at him, he eventually said, "Next time, I'll get some of that gross fiber stuff that you

263

like."

"It's not gross. It's good for you," I insisted. "Are you almost ready to go? We've got to be there in thirty minutes."

"I've been ready. You're the one in here searching through all the kitchen cabinets for something to eat."

"I was hungry!"

He placed his hand on my ever-so-large and growing-by-the-minute belly. "You're always hungry, Sunshine."

I rolled my eyes and said, "It's your fault, you know. With your gene pool, he'll probably end up being ten feet tall."

Clutch's lips curled into a mischievous grin as he asked, "You reckon he'll have big hands, too?"

Before I had a chance to respond, Charlie came barging into the kitchen and shouted, "I'm rolling out!"

"Wait!" I shouted. I rushed over and straightened his tie. I tried to hold back my tears as I said, "You look so handsome."

"Don't go getting all mushy on me, Sis. I've gotta go," he told me as he pulled away. He headed for the back door and yelled, "I'll see you there!"

"We better get moving," Clutch told me. "I'll grab Casey and meet you in the car."

"Okay," I told him as I grabbed a couple of snack bars and shoved them in my purse.

When we arrived, all of Clutch's brothers were already there waiting in the parking lot. I could tell by the expression on his face that it meant a lot to him that they were there. Even Cyrus came all the way from Memphis, and I was pleasantly surprised to see that he'd brought Sam along with him. When I'd last talked to him, he was about to be patched into the club, so I knew he had gotten back on his feet. I almost didn't recognize him with his bright-colored polo and khaki pants, but as soon as he smiled, I knew it was him.

I rushed over to him and gave him a big hug. "I can't believe you came! It's so good to see you!"

"I wouldn't miss it," he said softly. "You look beautiful, Olivia."

"Thanks, Sam. You look pretty great yourself," I told him as I linked my arm through his and led him towards the seating area. "Let's go find a place to sit."

It was a perfect afternoon. The sun was shining bright and there was a cool breeze whipping around us as we sat there waiting. I looked to my side, watching Clutch make funny faces at our daughter Casey. She was only eighteen months old but I could already tell that she was going to be just like her father, with her silly sense of humor and mischievous smiles, and I wouldn't have it any other way. Hadley was sitting next to them, texting on her phone as usual, and she looked absolutely stunning. I couldn't believe how much she'd grown in the past three years, and I just couldn't stop staring at her. When she noticed that I was looking at her, she rolled her eyes and pointed to the front as she said, "Charlie is about to come up."

Clutch

My heart swelled with pride as I watched my brother walk up to the podium. He'd worked so hard, and I knew it meant the world to him that he'd made valedictorian of his class. He stepped up to the microphone and smiled when he spotted us all sitting out in the crowd. The only thing missing was our parents. It was days like this that I missed them the most. They would have been so proud to see him standing up there in his cap and gown. Their children's education meant a great deal to them, so with the inheritance money, I'd paid Charlie's college tuition in full and bought him a safe vehicle to drive back and forth. I planned to do the same for Hadley when she graduated. As they stepped out to make their mark on the world, money would never be an issue for either of them; Dad made sure of that.

When the graduation ceremony was over, we all headed over to the clubhouse. The guys had a big barbeque planned and everyone was excited to celebrate Charlie's success. The brothers of Satan's Fury were our family, and they never failed to be there at our side whenever we needed them. With all of them, we'd found our home, and there was no other place I'd rather be.

The End.

Smokey's book is coming soon. And Blaze will also get his own book in the near future!

Acknowledgements

Marci Ponce – Your dedication astounds me. Thank you for always being there to give me that little push I need to make the book even better. I can't wait for you to publish your own book so I can do the same for you.

Amanda Faulkner – You are the world's best PA. I can't begin to thank you for all that you do. Please know that it means so very much to me and I couldn't do this without you.

Natalie Weston – Thank you for always being there to listen and give advice. Your friendship is truly a blessing.

Daryl and Sue Banner, The Dynamic Duo – Thank you for being patient with me during the editing process. I am sure I drove you both nuts, but you were always so very sweet. I love your work, and I loved your formatting. *If you haven't checked out Daryl Banner's books on Amazon, you are missing out. Try his latest book *Read My Lips*! It's awesome!

Clutch

Monica Langely Hollyway – Your teasers and banners are awesome. Thank you so much for bringing my quotes to life.

Neringa Neringiukas – You are the teaser guru. Thank you so much for sharing my book and teasers, and all of your kind words of support. You rock!

Ana Rosso – You've been with me since the beginning, and your support has meant so very much to me. I am so proud of you for writing your first book, Reaper's Creed MC. I'm sure it will be a smashing success.

Kaci Stewart, Danielle Deraney Palumbo, Tanya Skaggs, Lisa Cullinan, Terra Oenning, and Patricia Ann Bevins – Thank you so much for always being there with your kind words and support. You ladies are awesome.

Wilder's Women – I am always amazed at how much you do to help promote my books and show your support. Thank you for being a part of this journey with me.

A Special Thanks to Mom – Thank you for always being there to read, chapter by chapter, giving me your complete support. I love you so very much, and it means the world to me that you that you love my characters as much as I do.

Sneak Peek

Cotton

Satan's Fury MC

Book 3

Prologue

My father always said it took a strong man to admit his mistakes, and an even stronger man to learn from those mistakes. The crazy thing was I never saw him make a mistake. Everyone looked up to my father, especially me. He was the kind of man who thought a handshake was enough; and where he was concerned, it was. He never broke his word, even when it was difficult to follow through. He never failed to provide for his family, giving us a life where we all felt safe and loved. He adored my mother with a passion that never seemed to waiver, making us all love him even more. I wanted to be just like him, but it just wasn't in the cards for me.

Born towheaded and full of mischief, I was the oldest of three sons. My dad got a kick out of my snow-white hair and nicknamed me Cotton, saying that one day I'd prosper just like the cotton fields in Tennessee. Even when my hair turned dark brown like his own, the nickname stuck. There was no doubt I held a special place in my father's heart; we could all see it. His eyes gleamed with pride whenever I was around. I knew he had high expectations for me, wanting me to be a good role model for my brothers, Joseph and Lucas; but more times than not, I found myself in some kind of trouble I had no business getting into. I just couldn't stop myself. It was nothing for us to sneak off in the middle of the day when we were supposed to be helping out at the house; or in the middle of the night when we should've been sleeping soundly. There was nothing better than running amuck with my brothers; and with them falling close behind, I sought to discover all the secrets the world had hidden within her. There wasn't a tree tall enough or a cave dark enough to deter my curiosity. While Joe and Luke would stand by watching, I'd slip into the dark depths of a cave, unaffected by the voice inside my head that screamed for me to turn back. I got a rush from the danger that lurked inside, drawing me in, deeper and deeper into the darkness. Maybe it had something to do with being the first-born son, or maybe it was just a part of who I was, but nothing could stop that restless feeling I felt stirring in my gut. More times than not, my brothers and I found ourselves in a heap of trouble, and there was nothing worse than seeing that look of disappointment in my father's eyes when we screwed up. Unfortunately, it happened a lot; but it didn't prevent us from doing it time and time again, knowing our father would always be there to help pull us out of trouble… until the day he wasn't.

When my father died, a part of me died with him, and the direction of my life changed forever. As I grew older, I always tried to remember what he said about being a strong man... a good man. In the life I've lived, I have made my mistakes—lots of them—but I've never had a problem admitting when I fucked up. The hard part wasn't learning from the mistakes I'd made; it was finding a way to fix them.

Chapter 1
Cotton

Sophomore Year of High School

I was fourteen when my father shocked us all by dying of a massive heart attack. His death damn near destroyed our family, ending the safe and secure world I'd always known. My mother hadn't worked in years, making it difficult for her to find a job that could sustain the life we'd grown accustomed to. When she'd finally managed to find a few odd jobs, it just wasn't enough, and I was overcome with the need to protect my mother and brothers. I loved them and couldn't stand to see the worry in their eyes. I knew I had to do something, anything to make things better for them. I started mowing lawns and running the local paper route, helping out the only way I knew how. I was doing all I could, and we were still barely able to pay our bills.

That's when my Uncle Saul stepped in, helping out in a way I couldn't.

Until then, I really didn't know much about my uncle, other than he was the president of some motorcycle club. I didn't know why we never spent time with him or his family, but I'd gotten the impression a long time ago that it had something to do with my mother. A look of disgust would cross her face whenever my dad mentioned his brother's name or his club, and eventually, he just stopped talking about him altogether. It was obvious to all of us she didn't care for him or what he represented, but at the time, she was in no position to turn down his offer to help. I never did understand her distaste for him. I liked Saul from the start. I could see my father when I looked into his eyes or heard his voice, reminding me of that secure feeling I had whenever my dad was around. I felt a pull to my uncle, and each time he'd come by the house, I'd stare out the window and watch as he pulled up on his motorcycle. There was a mystery to him that intrigued me, making me want to know more about his life and his club that existed on the outside of town

Years passed, and even though I knew my mother wouldn't approve, I asked my uncle if he could help me find a more substantial job, thinking the money would help out with the bills. I'd heard him talking about a house renovation the club was doing for one of their members, and since I was good with my hands, I hoped he'd be able to find a place for me. When I brought it up to Uncle Saul, I figured he would say no because of my age, but I knew I had my father's build which made me look older than I really was, so I took a chance. At first he hesitated, but after I explained it would really help us out and promised to keep up my grades up at school, he finally agreed. It didn't take me long to realize the job I so desperately wanted wasn't exactly what I thought it would be. Since I was much younger than any of the club members, they had me doing all the grunt work that they didn't want to do themselves. I'd never worked harder in my life, but I liked being there, working with all of those men my uncle called his brothers, and soon began to feel like I was a part of something more than just a work crew. I felt like I belonged, especially when they'd let me tag along on some of their rides to blow off steam after work. Being on a bike with them was all that I thought it would be and more. The only thing better would have been having one of my own.

I'd been working with them for almost six months—we had finished one brother's house and had moved on to the next—when my cousin, Derek, showed up on the work site, and as soon as he stepped out of his truck, it was clear to us all he was on a war path. At first glance, he reminded me a lot of Uncle Saul with his tall, thick build and coal-black hair, but unlike his father, his greenish-blue eyes showed no warmth behind them. I watched as he stormed over to Doc with his fists clenched and a scowl on his face, all the while grumbling curses under his breath. Doc wasn't the kind of man who took shit from anyone, especially some angry kid. He was a retired military medic, and he expected respect, and he always received from his crew. After a brief one-sided argument, Derek's face flashed red with anger. While grumbling under his breath, he grabbed one of the tool belts off of the table and walked over to me. He gave me a quick grunt and chin lift, then immediately got to work. It was almost an hour later before he ever actually spoke to me.

"You actually *wanted* to work here with these fuckers?" he asked with a frustrated look.

"Yeah. Guess I did," I confessed.

"You got a screw loose or something?" he huffed. He didn't wait for me to answer before he said, "Pop's all pissed 'cause I got pulled over for speeding last night. It wouldn't have been a big deal if that nosy ass cop hadn't gone digging in the back of my truck and found the cooler of beer and my bag of pot. He blew a gasket when he had to bail me out of jail again. Told me I had to work out here as my fucking punishment, but the old man's got another thing coming if he thinks I'm going do this shit for free," he complained.

"That's a tough break," I responded, not really knowing what to say.

"Ah, hell. This isn't the first time, and it won't be the last," he laughed. I looked over at him, noticing the mischievous smirk that spread across his face. There was something about that look that set me on edge, but I quickly forgot about it when he said, "You should come out with me and the guys tomorrow night. Some of us are heading over to Mindy's party after the football game."

I was only a sophomore at the time and spent most of my time working or helping my mother out with my brothers, so I hadn't gone to many high school parties. I couldn't help but get a little excited about going to one of Mindy's blowouts. Trying not to sound too eager, I said, "Yeah, that'd be cool. I'll just meet you at the game."

I spent the next few hours listening to Derek gripe and groan as we finished the last of the demolition. By the time I finally made it home, I was beyond exhausted, and it was all I could do to take a shower before I crashed for the night. The next day, everybody was hyped up about the party. It was all anyone was talking about, and by the time we pulled up at Mindy's house, the place was packed. The music was blaring through the house as I followed Derek and his buddies through the crowd and into the kitchen. We shuffled through the different groups of popular kids, each one totally absorbed in their own conversation, until we passed a couple of seniors. They glared at Derek as he passed by them, making it known to everyone they weren't happy about him being there, but Derek didn't care. He didn't give a shit what anyone thought of him, and it showed. He had an air of confidence that was almost too much for me to bear, but his friends ate it up, laughing and carrying on right along with him. They were like a pack of wild dogs sniffing through the crowd, marking their territory along the way, and I found myself wishing I'd skipped the party altogether.

We'd been there for almost an hour when Derek came over to me and asked, "You ready for another one?"

I was on my fourth beer and already feeling a buzz when he handed me another full cup. With a wicked grin, he pulled out several pills from his back pocket and dropped them into his drink. After swirling it around for a few seconds, he said, "I'll be right back."

I was surprised to see that he was heading over to Sara Locke, one of the girls from the club. Her father was one of the brothers of Satan's Fury, but that didn't seem to slow him down. In fact, from the way he was eye fucking her, he obviously had a thing for her. Sara was a little younger than most of the girls at the party, but she was by far the most attractive around. She was wearing a short skirt with black cowboy boots and a sweater with a slight V, showing off all of her curves. Her long, dark hair fell loose around her shoulders and barely covered her breasts. There was no doubt about it—she was a fucking knockout. When Sara noticed Derek walking in her direction, she glared at him suspiciously, her fierce, blue eyes watching his every move. A lustful smile spread across Derek's face as he approached her and offered her his drink. She hesitantly took the drink from his hand and seemed leery as she studied what was inside the cup. For several seconds,

she just held the cup in her hand, swishing it from side
to side, but when her friend encouraged her to take a
drink, all of her doubts were quickly forgotten. Just as
she brought the cup to her mouth, Derek glanced back at
me and winked, giving me an evil grin. He continued to
talk to Sara and her friends for a few more minutes, then
he playfully swatted her on the ass before strutting back
over to me.

"What the fuck did you just do?" I barked.

"Relax, man. I just got the party started, brother," he
snickered. "Nothing better than easy pussy."

"You fucking drugged her?" I roared.

"Fuck, yeah, I did. Now keep your damn voice
down."

"Look, man, I've got no problem if the chick is
willing, and hell, Sara looks hot tonight... damn hot. I'd
be all over that shit, but taking what hasn't been offered
isn't an option."

"Didn't realize you were such a fucking tight ass,
Cotton. Guess I was wrong about you after all," he
huffed, then turned back to his buddies, bragging once
again about what he'd just done.

Everyone except Derek's crew seemed completely
unaware of what had taken place, which pissed me off
even more. I couldn't take my eyes off Sara, but I
wasn't the only one. Derek was watching her like a
hawk, waiting for his drugs to kick in. Seeing the
hungry look in his eyes when he ogled her repulsed me
even more. The guy had no honor, no reservations about

what he was doing, and I hated him for it. I had no idea how many girls had come before Sara, but I refused to let him get away with it again. Along with one of Derek's sidekicks, I noticed that her eyes were glassing over and her balance was off, but I caught my break when several girls approached Derek and his buddies. They were momentarily distracted and didn't see Sara when she started staggering toward the stairs. Knowing it might be my only chance to help her, I cautiously followed and found her in Mindy's parents' room. I'd prayed Derek had just been fucking around, but when I found Sara's lifeless body sprawled out across the bed, there was no doubt he'd drugged her. She was completely out of it, and I knew I had to do whatever I could to protect her.

When I heard Derek's voice drawing closer, I rushed over and locked the door. I turned back, glancing at Sara lying there on the bed, and it was all I could do to keep from slamming my fist through the wall. I wanted to stomp Derek's ass, but unfortunately, I knew I couldn't take him on with all of his buddies in tow. There were just too many of them and they weren't the type to fight fair. When I heard the taunting shouts of my name vibrating through the walls, I knew I had to act fast. Trying to buy myself some time, I grabbed a chair and propped it against the door, bracing it firmly, so no one could get in.

The doorknob turned and jolted, and when it didn't open, Derek started pounding on the door. "Cotton, I know your ass is in there. Open the fucking door."

"Not going to happen, *Derek*. Just back the hell off," I roared.

"You've got thirty seconds to open this goddamn door, or I am going to knock the motherfucker down," he barked.

"Yeah... you go ahead and do that. Won't take any time for everyone to come running to see what's going on up here. Either way, this thing with you and Sara isn't gonna happen," I scoffed.

"The hell it isn't! She's mine, motherfucker, and there's nothing you can do to stop me from having her!" he shouted as his fist slammed into the door once again. "Open the fucking door!... Fuck! You're dead, Cotton! Dead!"

Knowing I was running out of time, I picked up the house phone and dialed 911. When I heard the operator answer, I laid the receiver on the bed next to Sara, rushed over to the window, and slipped out onto the roof.

As soon as my feet hit the ground, I heard someone shout, "*There he is! Hey, Derek. He's out back.*"

I knew things were about to go south, so I took off running, hoping like hell I might have a chance to make it to the railroad tracks before they could catch me. I was wrong, and it cost me. I'd barely made it a half a mile down the road when Derek's truck pulled up next to me, and one of the guys jumped out and tackled me to the ground. Even though he was much bigger than me, I managed to get back on my feet, but in a matter of seconds, all six of them were on top of me. I did my best to fight them off, but it was difficult with all of them coming at me at once. I was holding my own until Derek slammed some kind of board across my chest, cracking several of my ribs with the force of the hit. When he hit me with it again, the pain got to be too much, and I dropped to my knees, unable to defend myself any longer. After that, everything was just a blur. Their grunts echoed around me as they plowed their feet into my side, chest, back, and head over and over again. I was just about to pass out when I heard police sirens coming down the road toward Mindy's house.

"Fuck! Get in the damn truck," Derek barked.

"You're just gonna leave him here?" one of them asked. "Shouldn't we take him off somewhere so nobody can find him?"

"We don't have time. Get your ass in the truck," he ordered.

I'm not sure how long I lay out there in the dark before Doc found me. I barely remember anything after Derek's truck drove off down the road, leaving me there to die. I woke up the next day in a room I'd never seen before, feeling like I had been put through a fucking meat grinder. Doc was standing over in the corner, talking to Uncle Saul, and I could see the concern in their eyes as they spoke.

When Uncle Saul looked over to me and saw I was awake, he walked over to the bed and rested his hand on my shoulder as he said, "You're gonna be okay, Cotton. Doc found you lying on the side of the road on his way in this morning. He almost passed you by, thinking you were some drunk, but when he saw that Mariner's baseball jacket of yours, he realized it was you. He was just going to take you on home until he saw the condition you were in."

I tried to sit up on the bed, but stopped when a pain shot through my side. Fuck. They'd done quite a number on me. My left eye was almost swollen shut, and my entire body was covered with bruises. I started to feel a little dizzy, so I laid my head back down on the pillow. Knowing I would've been in even worse shape if it weren't for Doc, I turned to him and said, "Thanks, Doc. Appreciate you helping me out."

"No problem, kid. You took one hell of a beating last night. Glad I came across you when I did."

As soon as he left the room, Uncle Saul said, "Just so we're clear. I know what happened last night. All of it. Sara's still a little out of sorts, but she'll be fine. Luckily, her father is a brother of the club, so the situation has been dealt with. And Derek... he will be dealt with as soon as I leave here. You can count on that." He took a deep breath, then continued, "You did good helping Sara last night. Glad you were there. She's family, and we do what we can to protect what's ours. You're already showing you can be trusted to do just that. Now, get some rest. I'll be back to check on you in a few hours."

Just before he walked out the door, I called out to him. "Uncle Saul... what about my mom? She was expecting me home last night and she's ..."

"Don't worry about her. Just get some rest and plan on staying here at the club for the rest of the weekend. I'll come up with something to tell your mother," he assured me.

I spent the next few days mending and learning my way around the clubhouse. I often worried about what was going on at home, but Uncle Saul assured me that my mom and brothers were fine. He'd told her I was helping one of the brother's out with a side job, and he'd make sure I got to school on Monday. I had no idea how he got her to go along with it—I was just glad he did. While I was there, I decided to make the best of it. I'd always wanted to know what it was like at the club, and since I was going to be staying for several days, I finally had my chance to see it for myself. Being there was everything I thought it would be and more. The clubhouse wasn't just a place to meet and drink beer, or even a place to work—it was home. The guys treated me like I was one of their own, and I found myself wanting to stay... even if I had to deal with Derek. I kept expecting to run into him, but he never showed. Later, I found out Uncle Saul had been true to his word, and Derek had been punished. After one hell of a beating from Sara's dad, Uncle Saul cut him off, telling him he wouldn't get another dime from him until he cleaned up his act. That never happened. Instead, he'd

Cotton

stolen money from a notorious drug dealer on the east side of town, and the trouble with Derek only escalated from there. He was set on a path no one could deter him from, and in the end, it cost him everything.

Get the rest of *Cotton*,
Book 3 in the Satan's Fury series,
on Amazon!

Made in the USA
Middletown, DE
10 January 2019